SENIOR THEATRE CONNECTIONS

The first directory of
Senior Theatre
performing groups,
professionals, and
resources

by
Bonnie L. Vorenberg

an

ArtAge
Publication

Portland, Oregon

Printed on acid free paper.

10   9   8   7   6   5   4   3   2

Published in the United States of America by ArtAge Publications, P.O. Box 12271, Portland, Oregon 97212-0271.

Printed in Canada

Library of Congress Cataloging-in-Publication Data.

Vorenberg, Bonnie L.
    Senior theatre connections: the first directory of senior theatre performing groups, professionals and resources / by Bonnie L. Vorenberg - 1st ed.
      p.cm.
    Includes bibliographical references and index.
    ISBN: 0-9669412-0-9

    1. Theater—Directories. 2. Theater and the aged—Directories. 3. Arts and the aged. 4. Aged—recreation—Directories. I. Title.

PN3160.A34V67 1999   799'.022'0846
      QB199-217

*M*y work in senior theatre would not have been possible without the support of teachers at the University of Oregon, such as Horace Robinson and Carl Carmichael who encouraged students to pursue the topic. I was later guided by talented colleagues such as Pauline Peotter, Paula Terry, Lisa Turpel, and others who realized the power of the field and gave their insight to aid its growth. Most importantly, I was sustained and inspired by the many seniors with whom I worked. Their talent, energy, and wonderful spirits were delightful both in rehearsal and on stage!

Research for this book was aided by Harold Cohen, Ann McDonough, Vicki Coffman, Joy Reilly, and others who continually supplied me information about senior theatre activity. I am deeply indebted to Janis Emerson, Julie Meyer, Dick Mort, and many others who gave their guidance and helped me realize the look and styling of the book. Finally, my appreciation goes to the Regional Arts and Culture Council for their support of this project and senior arts, in general.

My work in senior theatre would not have been possible without the special support and encouragement from Damien Brard, Dorothee Postel, Beauregard, and especially, from Robert Dupuy and his lifelong dedication.

Notes

Every attempt was made to insure accuracy of the data, but some names, addresses, and contact information may have changed since the production of this book.

Senior theatre is a rapidly expanding field with new groups and professionals becoming active daily. If you are interested in knowing more about current events in Senior Theatre, contact *ArtAge Publications* to be added to the mailing list at P.O. Box 12271, Portland, Oregon 97212-0271. ✫

Illustration by Janis Emerson
Book Design by Julie Meyer

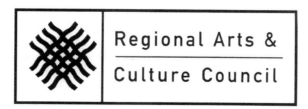

*S*enior Theatre Connections is the first directory to compile information about the groups, professionals, and resources which are contributing to the field of senior theatre and performing. It is a comprehensive exploration of who is working and what is successful. The directory brings all the elements together in one location—from funding sources to books and other resources. Handy and concise, the directory also points readers to opportunities such as community theatres, arts agencies, and associations. Even playwrights and publishers working to expand the literary offerings are included.

This directory provides information for all levels of performers—from beginning to advanced and will be useful for those who are working in a care center or on stage with a professional company—it has handy and useful information and offers something for everyone. The information spans the entire field, includes music and dance, and ranges from the basics in improvisation to acting in films and commercials.

Senior Theatre Connections is a tool for practitioners. It will encourage readers to expand or initiate performing programs for seniors. In addition, the directory will be a useful tool for young professionals who are exploring senior theatre as a vital career choice.

Senior theatre gives to everyone, from participants to audiences. It is physically and mentally stimulating, as well as being socially relevant. Whether older actors have been performing their entire lives or are newcomers to the footlights, being on stage brings a new lease on life. Even the camaraderie formed by a theatre 'family' helps promote health and wellness. But it is the forum of theatre which is so dynamic for elders. On stage, they can convey their thoughts, feelings, hopes, and dreams to future generations while audiences cheer them on!

Senior Theatre Connections demonstrates the depth and vitality of senior theatre and performing and encourages others to get involved, leading them down the yellow brick road of discovery. ☆

Bonnie L. Vorenberg

TABLE OF
CONTENTS

Dedication & Notes iii

Preface v

Foreword ix

Introduction to Performing Groups 3

Performing Groups in the United States 7

Performing Groups in Canada 33

Performing Groups in Europe & Other Countries 37

Performing Artists & Presenting Organizations 43

Professionals in Senior Theatre 47

Publishers, Playwrights & Scripts 51

Other Opportunities in Senior Theatre 65

      Academic Programs 66

      Acting in Commercials 67

      Education Programs in Theatre 68

      Reminiscence & Interactive Theatre 71

Community Theatres with Senior Programs 75

Associations in Arts & Aging 83

Senior Theatre Films & Videos 87

Funding for Senior Theatre 93

Bibliography of Books, Play Anthologies & Articles 109

Index 117

      Alphabetical 117

      Geographical 125

I'll never forget walking into my first senior theatre classroom in 1977. I was expecting to find a group of crotchety women, bent over and barely walking with depressed attitudes and frowns on their faces. Instead, I was in for the shock of my life.

The women I found in the *"One Nighters"* broke all the stereotypes of growing older. As a Graduate Student at the University of Oregon studying theatre and gerontology, I wondered, what was wrong with the books I was reading because these folks surely didn't fit the mold!

Actually, what I found with the *"One Nighters"* seems to be consistent for senior theatre. It is an art form which attracts a vibrant group of individuals who demonstrate talent, courage, intellect, a willingness to meet challenges, and a heightened sense of fun. They revel in seeing themselves on stage in colorful or comedic costumes and have a tendency to live fully with an optimistic outlook towards life, enjoying a group experience, and thrilling to the sound of applause.

I have had many years to come to these conclusions. I worked with the *"One Nighters"* for three years appearing before audiences throughout the Eugene, Oregon area. The company continues to be active and is now the *Encore Theatre*, a senior theatre for youth. It gives me intense pleasure to know that the group is still in existence!

Later, I moved to Portland, Oregon and formed an organization called *Arts for Elders*, a training institute for seniors and the arts. Through that work, I was able to locate actors, singers, and dancers who constituted the *Oregon Senior Theatre*. Organized in 1983, the group began with a cast of twelve which presented over 30 shows of *"Starting Here, Starting Now,"* in their first season. Each year, we produced a new production on different topics, continually performing 40 to 50 shows in a strenuous nine-month season.

One of our featured productions was *"Finishing Touches,"* a life review play about growing older, with over 40 performers and crew. It was presented at the 1989 National Council on Aging Annual Meeting in New Orleans before taking it on a midwest tour of Indiana and Illinois.

Touring was the way we did our work. We 'schlepped' costumes, props, sound, and scenery to every site. New stages, new everything, each show required adjustments. One time, the bus driver who was taking us to a show outside Chicago, missed the turn off. Because we were going to have no time to set up, everyone in the cast changed their clothes on the bus! They were troupers!

Usually we travelled within Oregon and Washington, but for three years in a row we received grants from the National Endowment for the Arts to perform in rural areas, spreading the word about senior theatre. In addition, we were selected to appear at Expo '86 in Vancouver, B.C., Canada. One year, we received 47 standing ovations in a row!

We took fund-raising to a new level. From yard sales, to knife sales, we learned how to run raffles, and even hold benefits at the local drag club! Our grant writing proved more and more valuable as our reputation spread.

Meanwhile, *Arts for Elders* established a talent agency for mature actors. Our seniors appeared in locally and nationally released movies, films, and commercials, as well as being featured in print ads and slide tape presentations. One even appeared on billboards. It was a thrill!

During the existence of the *Oregon Senior Theatre*, the round-the-clock work took a toll, causing me to hire my replacement—one of the most painful experiences of my life. But the group continues as the *Northwest Senior Theatre*—some of the seniors have spent eighteen of their retirement years performing on stage!

The same spirit that fueled my prior work was sparked again when I talked with the many directors and performers who glow with the same sense of enthralled enthusiasm! It has been a joy discovering them and seeing the intense growth in this new genre of theatre. I hope their stories will inspire you to explore the field and reap the many rewards which come when seniors are in the spotlight! ☆

One Nighters appear in "Hallulejah, I'm a Bum."

OREGON SENIOR THEATRE

The author, Bonnie L. Vorenberg (center)
with the Oregon Senior Theatre performers.

SENIOR THEATRE CONNECTIONS

by
Bonnie L. Vorenberg

INTRODUCTION TO PERFORMING GROUPS

cross this country and around the world, seniors are experiencing the thrill of being on stage! The quickly expanding movement is both introducing new performers and expanding the opportunities for those who have already accomplished the basics. From fully staged productions with all the lights, sound, and costumes, to small productions relying on puppetry or life stories, the one thing in common is that the groups are very busy, wildly successful, and most even have their own following of groupies!

By watching seniors on stage, it is obvious that they benefit from the experience. Their faces shine with enthusiasm, their bodies move to the music, and their efforts are rewarded by hearty applause. But much more is derived from the experience. Not only are seniors involved in an activity which stimulates both body and mind and fosters creativity, but a social network develops, one which is filled with caring and sharing–an element which is often lacking in the lives of older people. It all builds commitment, a sense of being needed, and an acceptable way of expressing the thoughts and feelings derived from many decades well lived.

Senior Theatre takes many forms. Often, several art forms are combined to create productions which meet the style and mission of the organization. As director of the *Oregon Senior Theatre*, we utilized theatre, music, and dance to create productions which followed a theme, such as *Finishing Touches*, which celebrated the joy of aging, or others which focused on radio, the '1930's', or Oregon history.

Each senior theatre company or program usually begins by selecting a style which best suits their talent or the mission of the organization. Once determined, the groups offer programs which range from oral history to readers theatre; from variety shows to intergenerational activities;

from issue-oriented productions to those which promote cultural awareness. What emerges are playwrights, stars, and a great deal of enthusiasm.

Many groups begin their work centering on life review or reminiscence. Some utilize it in classroom experiences which lead to improvisation; others develop it further by using memories as the basis for fully staged productions.

In readers theatre, groups often turn to literature, life stories, or local history for performance content. This type of production can be done simply by having participants seated while they act, reading from a printed script, or can be fully staged using lighting, movement, and scenery.

By far, the most common form of performance in senior theatre is the variety show. Though some groups feature a small company of eight to ten performers, others use a very large cast recruited from the community. This type of production combines theatre, music, dance, and costumes, creating spectacle and a great deal of theatrical effect.

Though aging is a very common thread for many productions, some organizations utilize it as their primary focus. When combining the message of aging with cultural awareness, stimulating theatrical offerings emerge. Other groups have selected intergenerational work while still others use history. Whatever the topic, well rehearsed and colorful productions take the audience through many emotions, often resulting in standing ovations!

Most of the performing groups are nonprofit organizations and are often sponsored by a wide range of organizations with senior centers, community colleges, universities, and park and recreation districts being the most common. They offer classes which span from beginning acting to complete productions which can bring in large amounts of capital. Sometimes, senior theatre funds some of the sponsor's work, pays for scholarships, or simply is used for expenses and to secure the future of the group.

Because the performers tour extensively, senior theatre is an excellent source of positive and inspiring public relations... usually successfully, because the media loves seniors on stage!

Why does senior theatre work? Performers benefit, taxpayers see their money put to good use, and the younger generation suddenly has an emotional way to reconnect with their elders. On a personal level, nothing does more to improve the perception of aging than to see an older parent, neighbor, or friend performing with gusto that belies their age. As the senior theatre movement grows, many more people will come to value the good things it does for the seniors involved, for the families, and for the society at large. ☆

This indicates the group is primarily a dance group.

PERFORMING GROUPS IN THE UNITED STATES

A.A.U.W. Readers Theatre
Evelyn Kyle
4 Reisling Court
Grand Junction, CO 81503
Phone: (970) 243-8927
Email: EEVEK@aol.com

Academy Theatre
Lorenne Fey
501 Means Street, NW
Atlanta, GA 30318
Phone: (404) 525-4111 / Fax: (404) 525-5659
Email: academytheatre@mindspring.com
Website: www.mindspring.com/
  academytheatre

Allan Lotsberg's NEW Fogey Follies
The Ford Center
420 North 5th St., Ste. 950
Minneapolis, MN 55401
Phone: (612) 359-9208

Apple Valley Players
Vern Harden
P.O. Box 78
Cedaredge, CO 81413
Phone: (970) 856-7430 / Fax: (970) 856-3577
Email: V_M_Harden@Hotmail.com

The Autumn Players
Deborah R. Austin
35 E. Walnut Street
Asheville, NC 28801
Phone / Fax: (828) 252-4723
Website: www.AshevilleTheatre.org
Sponsor: Asheville Community Theatre

Back Porch Dance Company
Joan Green and Victoria Solomon
51 Inman Street
Cambridge, MA 02139
Phone: (617) 492-8994 / Fax: (617) 441-9428
Email: greenbrown@erols.com
Website: www.backporchdanceco.org

Better Than Ever Independents, Inc.
The Better Than Ever Independents, Inc. were formerly affiliated with Robert Morris College. The group was organized in September 1990 for people 55 years of age and older who were interested in the performing arts. They performed several musical variety shows, dramas, and one-act plays at the college and appeared twice at Senior Theatre U.S.A. in Las Vegas, Nevada.

In 1997, the college closed their theatre, leaving the group without a sponsor. The members decided to reorganize and become independent. They have now incorporated as a nonprofit organization with a governing board.

In 1998, the group presented two successful dinner theatre shows and a third is scheduled for May, 1999. In addition, they perform for women's organizations, corporations, senior retirement communities, and nursing homes throughout Pittsburgh, Pennsylvania.

The Better than Ever Independents participated in the senior Theatre U.S.A. '99 at Disney World in Orlando, Florida with performances at the Omni Rosen Hotel and at the Galaxy Theatre in the Magic Kingdom. They received an award for their outstanding performance. Lou Valenzi is the Music Director for the group and Marta Zak is the accompanist. ☆

Better Than Ever Independents, Inc.
Ester R. Pavlis, President
516 Pine Road, Sewickley, PA 15143
Phone: (412) 741-7850 / Fax: (412) 741-2346

Anderson Senior Follies

Anderson Senior Follies is a thriving celebration of Senior Theatre with seventy novice senior performers from the Anderson, South Carolina area who write the scripts, perform, sing, dance, act, build sets, construct costumes, and market their musical extravaganza with professional determination. Productions typically involve over twenty-five musical numbers whereby everyone sings and dances (at the same time!) and up to two-hundred forty costumes have been created for a single production! The annual show is always the first weekend in March. Yet, in its ten-year existence, *Senior Follies* has evolved into a year-round organization with a governing board, professional outreach performances, and fundraising branches.

Senior Follies has enjoyed recognition at both the local and national levels, plays annually to sold-out houses and makes a profit of thousands of dollars each year. The funds raised are used to upgrade the performance facility at Anderson College, the sponsoring organization.

The energy of this polished and dynamic group is astounding and they attribute their success to a positive team effort which welcomes any senior fifty-five or over to be a part of the *Senior Follies* 'family.' Everyone who participates is featured, everyone is a star. A new script is written each year and every show is new and refreshing for both the performers and the audiences.

Members of the *Senior Follies* cast will tell you that it is a privilege to be a part of the group and that they are proud to share their talents. Even rehearsals are great fun – though they resemble the energy of a Richard Simmons workout. And, when opening night comes after an eight-week rehearsal run, every cast member lights up the stage with pride and enthusiasm as *Senior Follies* continues to be "*One Singular Sensation!*" ☆

• • • •

"I saw this group

perform at the Senior

Theatre Festival in

Orlando and their

standing ovation was

well deserved!

Outstanding!"

An Audience Member

> **"Once you get people laughing, they're listening and you can tell them almost anything."**
>
> *Herb Gardner*

Anderson Senior Follies
Annette Cantrell Epstein
Anderson College
316 Boulevard
Anderson, SC 29621
Phone: (864) 231-2080
Fax: (864) 231-2083
Email: epstein@carol.net

The Class Act

The Class Act offers nonstop entertainment through lively one-acts, each differing in tone, flavor, style and tempo. Songs are performed accompanied by piano and other musical instruments such as trumpet or trombone. Performances can be tailored to specific themes such as Oktoberfest, St. Patrick's Day, Valentine's Day, or to meet the needs of the sponsoring organization.

The Class Act performances are 50 fun-filled minutes of song, dance, and comedy. The repertory includes brief opera arias, selections from great musicals and operettas, ethnic dances, and more. They also can include line dancing and ballroom dance demonstrations.

The Class Act has performed for the National Theatre, the Montgomery County Recreation Department, and many other audiences earning them numerous repeat performances and high acclaim. ☆

The Class Act
Anna Pappas
8817 Copenhaver Drive
Potomac, MD 20854-3008
Phone: (301) 340-8723

Chula Vista Senior Citizen Club
Don Jones
270 F. Street
Chula Vista, CA 91910
Phone: (619) 691-5086

Communi-Culture Performing Arts Association
Barbara Rothman Vojta
P.O. Box 45945
Rio Rancho, NM 87174-5945
Phone: (505) 771-0143
Fax: (505) 771-0143 (please call first)
Email: BARBVOJTA@aol.com
Website:
www.Geocities.com/Broadway/Balcony/4185/
Sponsor:
NMREEF (New Mexico Research,
Education and Enrichment Foundation)

Concord Senior Citizens Club
Diane Lorenzetti
2727 Parkside Circle
Concord, CA 94579-2523
Phone: (925) 671-3320

Cradle to Grave Arts
Hannah Dennison
386 South Winooski Avenue
Burlington, VT 05401
Phone: (802) 864-4705
Email: hwd@together.net

Culver City Senior Center
4153 Overland Avenue
Culver City, CA 90230
Phone: (310) 253-6700

Curtain Time Players
Mary Jo Denolf
c/o RSVP 50 Weston
Grand Rapids, MI 49503
Phone: (616) 459-9509

Curtain Time Retirement Vignettes
c/o Robert Redd
P.O. Box 56
Ada, MI 49301
Phone: (616) 676-1583

The Dance Generators

Amie Dowling
80 Williams Street, #2B
Northampton, MA 01060
Phone: (413) 584-4329

Dance Wheels
Community Access to the Arts
Sandra Newman
P.O. Box 46
Stockbridge, MA 01262
Phone: (413) 298-4765

Drama Dears
Linda Bogan, Shirley Bridges
408 E. Marion Street
Shelby, NC 28150
Phone: (704) 482-3488
Sponsor: Cleveland Co. Council on Aging/
Senior Center

The Entertainers
Barbara Le Chaix
11402 S. Shoshone
Phoenix, AZ 85044
Phone: (602) 893-2976

• • • •

"Senior Theatre keeps me off the streets and out of the bars!"

Anita Reed, Oregon Senior Theatre and Northwest Senior Theatre performer, age 73

Encore Theatre

Encore Theatre, a senior theatre for youth, is a troupe of talented seniors that presents free, interactive shows for young people about aging, living, and learning. The shows are based on the troupe members' own lives. Through original songs, dance, and storytelling, the performers reach across the years to share themselves with their younger audiences.

Future plans include establishing *Encore* troupes in other towns around Oregon and other locations, teaching seniors how to integrate their stories into a framework and perform in local schools. *Encore* is a great opportunity for seniors to become involved with children, benefit their communities and celebrate their age! ☆

Encore Theatre
Eliza Roaring Springs
P.O. Box 50816
Eugene, OR 97405
Phone: (541) 342-1630
Email: elizars@earthlink.net

Extended Run Players

The Extended Run Players are a group of senior theatre artists who perform readers theatre pieces throughout San Antonio and the surrounding areas. The group was selected to appear at the 1998 convention of the Association for Theatre in Higher Education.

The group's repertory includes: *Dear Liar, You Can Never Have Too Much Sky – Readings From the Work of Sandra Cisneros, The Humor of Being Human*, and *The Little Prince*. They have performed on the University of the Incarnate Word campus and at local theatres and retirement facilities. Performances contribute to the Theatre Arts Scholarship Fund.

The Extended Run Players is a growing and dynamic group. The players bring their experiences and history to make their readers theatre stage come alive. ☆

Extended Run Players
Sister Germaine Corbin
c/o Theatre Arts Department
University of the Incarnate Word
4301 Broadway
San Antonio, TX 78209
Phone: (210) 829-3806
Fax: (210) 283-5026
Email: Corbin@universe.uiwtx.edu
Website: http://www.uiw.edu/theatre.html

Fabulous Palm Spring Follies

Housed in the historic Plaza Theatre in the Downtown Village of Palm Springs, the *Fabulous Palm Spring Follies* has entertained more than a million fans over the past seven years.

Featuring the music and dance of the 1930's and '40's, the group performs a nostalgic and professional razzle-dazzle extravaganza. Performances usually feature headliners such as Donald O'Connor, their Follies Man, Riff Markowitz, along with a signature line of "long-legged lovelies" (all 54 to 86 years young!) and spectacular sets and costumes.

The *Follies* usually have a lengthy season with both matinee and evening shows. The group was highlighted in an Academy Nominated Documentary, "*Still Kicking*." ☆

Fabulous Palm Spring Follies
Dan Jardin
128 S. Palm Canyon Way
Palm Springs, CA 92262
Phone: (760) 327-0225
Fax: (760) 322-3196
Email: PSFollies@earthlink.net
Website: www.PSFollies.com

Footsteps of the Elders

Footsteps of the Elders is an independent touring theatre troupe founded in 1994 and directed by Sarah Worthington. The highly innovative group works with their own reminiscences and creates performance works through improvisation. *Stone Soup*, the group's first play, collected scenes depicting the members from toddlers to high-school graduates. *From Clothesline to Online* traced their years since World War II and premiered in London, England at a conference for the European Reminiscence Network.

In 1996, a program for National Women's History Month helped focus *Footsteps* on womens' issues and concerns - an issue close to the hearts of the members, women aged 65 to 83 and living on fixed incomes. In a three-month residency, the group collaborated with teenagers to produce *Making Do*, a play about the Depression. Their next play, *Now You See Us, Now You Don't*, concerns 'invisible older women,' and how with age, the members are becoming more independent, better able to make their own decisions, and write their own rules.

Footsteps of the Elders works minimalistically, with black costumes, bare sets, and few or no props. The emphasis is on drama and character. All performances are ASL interpreted and diversity is welcomed.

Footsteps has been called controversial, honest, humorous, and passionate. The performers are life-experienced with wit, talent, and wisdom. ☆

Footsteps of the Elders
Sarah Worthington
693 Yaronia Drive
Columbus, OH 43214
Phone: (614) 262-2033
Fax: (614) 890-5220
Email: carter.3@osu.edu

The Fab Fifties Follies
Betsy Nein
P.O. Box 522521
Longwood, FL 32752
Phone: (407) 831-9991

Fountain Valley Seniors
Dennis Crosser
5745 Southmoor Drive
Fountain, CO 80817
Phone: (719) 520-6471

The Funsters
c/o Sidy Rayfeld
7747 Tommy Drive, E #15
San Diego, CA 92119
Phone: (619) 460-6539

Foxettes RiverCity Theater - Silver Foxettes and the Guys
Maxine Vanevenhoven
Summer (April 1 through November 1):
    108 Idlewild Street
    Kaukauna, WI 54130
    Phone: (920) 766-1828
Winter:
    620 Hidden River Drive
    Port St. Lucie, FL 34983
    Phone: (561) 879-1373

Full Circle Theatre
Rob Hutter
1601 N. Broad Street, #206
Philadelphia, PA 19122
Phone: (215) 204-3195
Fax: (215) 204-8559

Geritol Frolics

The Geritol Frolics, started in 1987, is the senior theatre program at Central Lakes College in Brainerd, Minnesota. Brainerd is located in central Minnesota, 120 miles northwest of the Twin Cities. The city has a population of 12,000 and the college has an enrollment of 3,000 students.

The Geritol Frolics is one of ten productions produced by the theatre department annually. They play to sold-out houses with tour groups traveling to performances in Brainerd from the Twin Cities and throughout Minnesota, as well as from Iowa, North Dakota, and Canada.

The production is famous for its dazzling costumes, snazzy scenery, and stylish staging. The cast size averages 50 members, ranging in age from 50 to 87. The production places an emphasis on intergenerational growth between traditional age theatre students and senior performers. ☆

Geritol Frolics
Dennis Lamberson
Central Lakes College
501 West College Drive
Brainerd, MN 56401
Phone: (218) 828-2371 / (800) 933-0346
Fax: (218) 828-2710

Grandparents Living Theatre

Grandparents Living Theatre is one of the best-known and most renowned senior theatre troupes. Founded in 1984 by Joy Harriman Reilly, the company has built a strong reputation based on their mission to "*celebrate life experience while shattering negative images of aging.*" They have appeared before audiences of all ages at colleges, schools, senior centers, hospitals, conferences, and conventions, always striving for the highest of artistic standards.

A professional company, the group has been honored as the headline conference opener for the National Council on Aging Conference and featured at the First International Senior Theatre Festival in Cologne, Germany. In addition, they have been recognized in numerous publications and on national television.

Grandparents Living Theatre has an ambitious schedule including performances, creating new works, and international projects. Their innovative **Poetry*Prose Company** is a professional readers theatre company which presents favorite selections of love poems in a production entitled, *From Grandparents with Love.*

Some of the plays which are on tour include: *"I Was Young, Now I'm Wonderful!"*; *"Picket Fence, Two Kids and a Dog Named Spot?"*; *"Woman"*; *"I Do! I do!"*; and *"I've Almost Got the Hang of It."*

The group is able to travel anywhere and the fees are negotiable. Several of the scripts are available for purchase. *Grandparents Living Theatre* has set a high standard of excellence which continues under the directorship of Executive/Artistic Director, Nancy Nocks. ✩

Above all, *Grandparents Living Theatre*
hopes to present theatre which speaks to
audiences of all ages with vision, humor,
and lasting impact." *Joy Reilly, Founder
and Artistic Consultant.*

"A highly professional troupe for which age
is merely an asset." *Harry B. Franklin,
Columbus, The Discovery City.*

Grandparents Living Theatre
Nancy S. Nocks
51 Jefferson Avenue
Columbus, OH 43215
Phone: (614) 228-7458
Fax: (614) 228-2052
Email: gplt@glt-theatre.org
Website: GLT-THEATRE.ORG

The Golden Troupers Readers Theatre And Singers
Chuck Shannon
4337 East Silver Springs Blvd.
Ocala, FL 34470
Phone: (352) 236-2274
Fax: (352) 236-0927 / Email: oct@pig.net
Website: www.ocalacivictheatre.com
Sponsor: Ocala Civic Theatre

"Gotta Dance!" Entertainment Troupe
Bob Burnham, Booking Agent
5311 Fleet Landing Blvd.
Atlantic Beach, FL 32233-4586
Phone: (904) 246-9079
Fax: (904) 246-9447 (Attn: Bob Burnham)
Sponsor: Fleet Landing Retirement Community

The Hauppauge Players
Harold Cohen
135 Atlantic Place
Hauppauge, NY 11788
Phone: (516) 234-9379

Highland Senior Players
Highland Senior Center
Jan DeLuna, Director
2880 Osceola
Denver, CO 80212
Phone: (303) 458-4868
Fax: (303) 458-4831

Horizon Senior Ensemble

Horizon Senior Ensemble is an avocational outreach program of Atlanta's Horizon Theatre Company, a professional theatre. Approximately twenty senior actor/playwrights create and perform original short plays based on discussion, improvisation, and journal writing. Topics reflect the interests and perspectives of senior adults. Previous experience in acting and playwriting is not required.

Led by *Horizon* co-artistic director Jeff Adler, the Ensemble debuts each new play at the Horizon Theatre, then performs at venues throughout Atlanta for groups of all ages. Ensemble members would like to network with similar groups and seeks scripts from playwrights. ☆

Horizon Senior Ensemble
Jeff Adler
Horizon Theatre Company
P.O. Box 5376
Atlanta, GA 31107
Phone: (404) 523-1477 / Fax: (404) 584-8815
Email: horizonco@mindspring.com
Website: www.mindspring.com/~horizonco/

• • • •

"I think it's important to show people our age how much it means to keep those creative juices flowing. Sometimes it's an effort, but at those times when you think, 'Shoot, why doesn't my body work like it used to?' you know it's well worth it because we always come out on a high when we are done. The eyes shine a little brighter when we walk out the door!" *Adiana Warner, Horizon Senior Ensemble member.*

Just Gotta Tap

Extension Dance Studio
Amy Alicea
3620 N.E. 8th Place, #7
Ocala, FL 34470
Phone: (352) 694-0601

Jeriatric Jubilee

Mt. Morris Senior Center
9 E. Front Street
Mt. Morris, IL 61054
(Please don't send scripts)
Phone: (815) 734-6335

The Kids on the Block, Inc.

Those involved with *The Kids on the Block, Inc. (KOB)* know that shaping attitudes isn't easy. Since the company was formed in 1977, they have developed more than 42 programs to enable enthusiastic individuals and groups worldwide to teach and inspire children through the magic of live puppet theatre.

The Kids on the Block, Inc. has troupes around the world. Many KOB performers have never picked up a puppet before. They can help you contact an existing troupe or start one of your own! ☆

To find out how, contact:

The Kids on the Block, Inc.
Elizabeth Dupree
9385-C Gerwig Lane
Columbia, MD 21046
Phone: (800) 368-KIDS (5437) or
   in Maryland: (410) 290-9095
Fax: (410) 290-9358
Email: kob@smart.net
Website: http://www.kotb.com

Lynnette Jelinek
4838 S.W. Scholls Ferry Road
Portland, OR 97267
Phone: (503) 246-5818
Email: kobl;@teleport.com

The Late Edition
Doug Stewart
One Cerrado Court
Santa Fe, NM 87505
Phone/Fax: (505) 466-4724
Email: Stewart@rt66.com
Sponsor: Top Down Motoring

Liz Lerman Dance Exchange

Art Weber, Booking Agent
7117 Maple Avenue
Takoma Park, MD 20912
Phone: (301) 270-6700 / Fax: (301) 270-2626
Email: artsource@compuserve.com

Merry Clements Players
Margaret D. Jenkins
12280 W. Alabama Place
Lakewood, CO 80228-3604
Phone: (303) 986-6462
Email: daisydog8@juno.com
Sponsor: Clements Community Center,
   City of Lakewood

Mooresville Senior Center
Sue McCrory
1601 SR 144
Mooresville, IN 46158
Phone: (317) 831-7510

New Castle Senior Activity Group
Roslyn Robinson
200 S. Greeley Avenue
Chappaqua, NY 10514

New Wrinkles Show
Tom Wright
1101 E. University Avenue
Fresno, CA 93741
Phone: (209) 442-4600, Ext. 8454
Fax: (209) 265-5729
Email: ctw02@alumni.CSUfresno.edu
Sponsor: Fresno City College

Northwest Senior Theatre
Vivian Lyman
P.O. 25624
Portland, OR 97298
Phone: (503) 251-4332

Off Washington Players
Thornton Senior Center
9471 Dorothy Blvd.
Thornton, CO 80233
Phone: (303) 451-1001

The Pearls of Wisdom
Elders Share the Arts
Susan Perlstein
72 East First Street
New York, NY 10003
Phone: (212) 780-1928
Fax: (212) 529-5062
Email: elderarts@aol.com

Penn State Goldenaires

Organized in September 1992, the *Penn State Goldenaires* have performed around the country. They appeared at the Senior Theatre Festival in 1993, 1995, 1997 in Las Vegas, and 1999 in Orlando, Florida. Under the direction of Professor Lillian Misko-Coury, the group has been actively presenting performances, even appearing at the UCL Conference in Station Square, among others. They are on the road appearing before at least nine outreach audiences every month.

Lillian Misko-Coury was responsible for the formation of the Senior Theatre Research and Performance Focus Group, a study area of the Association of Theatre in Higher Education which was organized in 1993. The national organization sponsors training sessions at the annual conference and guides the Senior Theatre Festival which is held every two years.

Penn State offers a wide variety of theatre classes for older performers. Seniors take classes ranging from acting, technical theatre, theatre production, to voice. They are able to earn a Continuing Education Certificate. ✩

Penn State Goldenaires
Lillian Misko-Coury
Penn State University Continuing Education
New Kenginston Campus
3550 7th Street. RD. Route 780
New Kensington, PA 15068
Phone: (724) 334-6716
Fax: (724) 334-6116
Email: lmc1@psu.edu

The Players Guild of Canton

Kris Furlan, Managing Director
1001 Market Avenue, North
Canton, OH 44702
Phone: (330) 453-7617
Fax: (330) 452-4477
Website: www.playersguildofcanton.com

Pontine Theatre

Marguerite Mathews
135 McDonough Street
Portsmouth, NH 03801
Phone: (603) 436-6660
Fax: (603) 436-1577
Email: pontine@nh.ultranet.com
Website: www.pontine.org

Port Ludlow Players
Dr. Robert Baker
Box 65308
Port Ludlow, WA 98365
Phone: (360) 437-2513

Prime Time Players
Mesa Senior Center
247 No. Macdonald
Mesa, AZ 85201
Phone: (602) 832-2027

Primus Theatre
Win O'Reilly
Studio Theatre
Chicago Cultural Center Renaissance Ct.
78 E. Washington Street
Chicago, IL 60602
Phone: (312) 744-4550 or
(312) 744-6630 (Cultural Affairs)

Queens Senior Safety Theatre Troupe
Queens Borough President's Office
Sara Pecker
120-55 Queens Blvd.
Kew Gardens, NY 11424
Phone: (718) 286-2663 / Fax: (718) 286-2916
Email: sarap@interpart.net
Website: www.queens.nyc.ny.us.graysafe
   http://members.aol.com/aaip/seniors.htm

Quincy Community Theatre
  Silver Stars
Barbara Rowell
300 Civic Center Plaza
Quincy, IL 62301
Phone: (217) 222-3209 / Fax: (217) 222-3188
Email: qct@rnet.com

The Raging Grannies of Seattle
P. Anna Johnson
P.O. Box 22048
Seattle, WA 98112
Phone: (206) 323-2187
Fax: (206) 323-2188
Email: grannies@raginggrannies.com
Website: www.raginggrannies.com

Return Engagement Players
Jules Abrams
2720 Blaine Drive
Chevy Chase, MD 20815-3042
Phone/Fax: (301) 585-9689
Email: jules368@juno.com
Sponsor: Montgomery County, MD

Sage Players
Kirsten Bonner
c/o Wild Space Dance Co.
P.O. Box 511665
Milwaukee, WI 53203
Phone: (414) 271-0712
Fax: (414) 271-6087
Email: kirs10lee@aol.com

Senior Barn Players
P.O. Box 12767
Shawnee Mission, KS 66282
Phone: (913) 381-4004

Seniors Reaching Out
Dr. Dorothy Perron
1050 Old Pecos Trail
Santa Fe, NM 87501
Phone: (505) 988-5522
Fax: (505) 988-2444
Email: srodp@aol.com

• • • •

**"Senior Theatre has given me
a lot of satisfaction and
most of all, the friends
I've made have changed my
life. I'm not married,
so they are my family."**

*Hugh Davis, Oregon Senior
Theatre & Northwest Senior
Theatre performer, age 75*

The Senior Class

The Senior Class, produced and directed by Peggy Lord Chilton, is a fast-paced, funny, sometimes poignant, always joyful two-act musical review now in its third financially successful year. Why reinvent the wheel? The director can put on the same show for you. Have music and choreography - will travel. ☆

The Senior Class
Peggy Lord Chilton
7777 E. Main Street, #129
Scottsdale, AZ 85251
Phone: (602) 946-3884

Peggy Lord Chilton, Director

• • • •

"If you feel old going into this show, you won't feel that way coming out." *Max McQueen, The Tribune.*

"...an enjoyable evening...doing some wonderful songs." *Jazz in Az Magazine.*

"All aglow...electric waves of excitement." *The New York Times.*

"The Senior Class is delightful." *Patricia O'Haire, The Daily News.*

Senior Players of American River Community (SPARC)

It is the artistic purpose of the *Senior Players of the American River Community (SPARC)* to provide quality theatrical experiences which explore the multifaceted issues of aging in the American society. Devoted to more than just performances, *SPARC* emphasizes learning and development in the theatrical process, the exploration of new dramatic forms, and the subsequent enrichment of the American River Community.

Past productions have included *Lysistrata; Encounters of a Third Age; We, the Memories:* and *The Women of Spoon River.* ☆

Senior Players of American River
   Community (SPARC)
Betty J. Francis
c/o Broadway Academy of
   Performing Arts
4010 El Camino Avenue
Sacramento, CA 95821
Phone: (916) 483-2775

The Seasoned Performers

The Seasoned Performers of Birmingham, Alabama, tour one-act plays and reading programs to audiences of senior adults and children in over 70 community sites each year. Since 1984, this active group of senior volunteer actors has been producing original material, providing performances opportunities for older adults, and bringing live theatre to special audiences reaching sites in up to ten Alabama counties each year. Theatre workshops are held periodically. *The Seasoned Performers*, under the auspices of the Jefferson County Council on Aging, a nonprofit service organization, originated in and is still partly supported by the Jefferson County Office of Senior Citizens Services. ☆

The Seasoned Performers
Martha Haarbauer
2601 Highland Avenue, So.
Birmingham, AL 35205
Phone / Fax: (205) 978-5095

Cast members of *"Fine Feathered Friends and the Rara Avie,"*
produced by *The Seasoned Performers.*

Senior Star Showcase

They sing, they dance, they act, and they love to perform...they're the *Senior Star Showcase*, and they're lighting up the stage at Essex Community College in Baltimore, Maryland.

In their 19th year of performing, the group consists of approximately 85 senior citizens between the ages of 55 and 75. Performing from September to June, they produce several shows a year, including two major Broadway musicals produced on campus and touring to three different venues from New York City to Washington D.C. and Las Vegas.

The *Senior Star Showcase* began in 1980 as the brainchild of Essex Professor Arne Lindquist, who continues to direct and orchestrate the productions. Knowing how much his father loved to dance, sing and act, Lindquist enlisted 15 older acquaintances and started a Senior Show Choir. After a few years, the group grew tired of singing around the piano. Lindquist then began to write musicals for them to perform. Eventually, as the company grew, their productions evolved into recognizable work such as, "*Guys and Dolls*" and "*Hello Dolly.*" ☆

• • • •

"**They feature a cast that's not getting older, but better.**" *WMAR, Channel 2*

"**They are living proof that it's never too late.**" *WMAR, Channel 2*

Senior Star Showcase
Arne Lindquist
Essex Community College
7201 Rossville Blvd.
Baltimore, MD 21228
Phone: (410) 780-6535

Sixty Karats

Sixty Karats is a group of performers who are all over the age of 60, with the average being 75 years old! Under the artistic direction of Jayne Letsche, the group has been performing for 11 years and has a repertore of over 20 tap dances, featuring percussion tap, soft shoe, as well as dances to boogie, jazz, and swing.

Sixty Karats has been appreciated by audiences throughout the United States including performances at the Kennedy Center in Washington D.C., the Grand Ol'Opry in Nashville, the Flamingo Hotel in Reno, Nevada, and the Grand Casino in Biloxi, Mississippi. They also performed at the Renaissance Hotel for the 1998 Annual Conference of The International Ticketing Association (INTIX) held in Washington D.C. They have appeared in television programs for CNN and CNN's Japanese affiliate. In 1998, they performed for the Smithsonian Associates program, "*Women of Tap*" with Ann Miller, and in 1999 for the Smithsonian program, "*Legends of Tap*" with Fred Kelly. Each summer, *Sixty Karats* are popular features on the boardwalk at Rehoboth Beach and Bethany Beach.

The women of *Sixty Karats* hope that both young and old alike who see their show-stopping performances will look upon them as inspiration, realizing that you are only as old as you feel! ✩

• • • •

"*The Sixty Karats*, **a group of dancing grandmothers, 'brought down the house' with their syncopated tap dancing. Watch out Rockettes!**" *Response to their performance at The International Ticketing Association as reported on their website.*

"**The Sixty Karats are awesome and will leave you breathless.**" *Quote from the Helen Hayes Gallery at the National Theatre, Washington D.C.*

Sixty Karats
Jayne Letsche, Director
6502 Cottonwood Drive.
Alexandri, VA 22310
Phone: (703) 971-5144
Fax: (703) 533-8749

Beverly Brown
Phone: (703) 534-3443
Email: brown@dc.net

Silver Wings Repertory Company

Ted Fuller
241 Greenwich Drive
Pleasant Hill, CA 94523
Phone/Fax: (925) 932-2049 (call first)
Email: TedPress@aol.com

Slightly Older Adult Players (S.O.A.P.)

Attn: Current President
1200 Raintree Drive
Fort Collins, CO 80526
Phone: (970) 221-6644
Sponsor: Fort Collins Senior Center

SPRI Theatre Company (Senior Players of Rhode Island)

Founded in 1995 by Steven Pennell, the company is a partnership of Brown University's Rites and Reason Theatre and the Smith Hill Center. The group works cooperatively with senior centers and schools throughout the state sharing their talent and experiences as they turn oral history into intergenerational performances.

Major projects included *"Meet Me At the Shepherd's Clock,"* a re-creation of the downtown holiday shopping experience of yesteryear as the windows of a former department store came alive to the fascination of hundreds of costumed shoppers who were being serenaded by street musicians.

Other productions included *"Just Women's Work,"* a multimedia/live performance piece with seniors and students, and *"Celebrate Community,"* with seniors and inner-city students in a movement theatre piece.

SPRI is funded by the University of Rhode Island Feinstein College of Continuing Education, City of Providence, in addition to numerous donors. Steven Pennell is a theatre professor and workshop leader on Senior Performance, Oral History as Performance, and Theatre as Healing. ☆

SPRI Theatre Company
Steven Pennell
Brown University
Box 1148
Providence, RI 02912
Phone: (401) 863-1815
Fax: (401) 863-3559

SPRI Theatre Company performing "Meet Me at the Shepherd's Clock."

Stagebridge

Stagebridge is the nation's oldest senior theatre. Founded in 1978 by Dr. Stuart Kandell, the company's mission has always been to provide opportunities for older adults to use theatre as a way to bridge the generations. The company consists of fifty actors, storytellers, students and volunteers whose average age is 70. *Stagebridge* has performed for over 130,000 people. Programming consists of a theatre training program with weekly classes in acting, storytelling, improv, and scene study; touring short plays to senior facilities and community sites; public performances of original plays about aging; an extensive intergenerational literacy program with local schools consisting of annual student matinee performances of our *Grandparents Tales* play; the Storytellers in the Schools Program which recruits, trains, and places older adults as storytellers in one of their partner schools, and the Storytelling Assembly Programs for local schools.

In 1997-98, the company gave 75 performances of four original plays *(Love, Sex and Growing Old, Caring; Grandparents Tales; It's Never Too Late!)* as well as 130 workshops for 19,050 people in schools, rest homes, hospitals, libraries, senior centers, and theatres throughout the San Francisco Bay area. The company continues to be run by founders Dr. Stuart Kandell and co-director/ playwright Linda Spector, with a small part-time staff. A part-time outreach coordinator regularly speaks at community sites. *Stagebridge* produces quarterly newsletters for 3,000 subscribers and is regularly featured in the local media. Forty-two percent of the income is earned from public and student matinee performances and touring fees, and 58% is contributed from sources such as the National Endowment for the Arts, Toyota USA, Mervyn's, Target, Wells Fargo, local foundations and 150 'Friends of Stagebridge.' Materials available for purchase include *Pass it On, a Programming Guide to Starting a Storytellers in the Schools Program* and *Stagebridge Storytellers on Radio*, and other publications. ✩

• • • •

"The work you are doing is very important."
The late Jessica Tandy.

"The fact that these seniors are up on stage sharing stories about their lives makes Stagebridge one of the most vital and authentic community theatre projects around. *Chad Jones, Oakland Tribune*.

"Empowering the elderly in tandem with children is a brilliant way to rebuild valuable and critically needed bridges between generations." *Children's Advocate Newspaper*

Stagebridge
Stewart Kandell
2501 Harrison Street
Oakland, CA 94612
Phone: (510) 444-4755
Fax: (510) 444-4821
Email: staff@stagebridge.org
Website: www.stagebridge.org

● ●

Still Acting Up!
Win O'Reilly
2217 W. Montrose
Chicago, IL 60618
Phone: (773) 539-7720

Southeast Focal Point Senior Center
3081 Taft Street
Hollywood, FL 33021
Phone: (954) 966-9805

Teatro NACE (Nuevos Actores and Cultura Expresiva)
Victor M. Salas
El Pasco Community College
Upward Bound Program
El Paso, TX 79915
Phone: (915) 833-9333 / Fax: (915) 833-9390

Theatre Works' Golden Troupers
Julia Thomson/Lynne Ormandy
9850 W. Peoria Avenue
Peoria, AZ 85345
Phone: (602) 815-1791 (Office)
(602) 815-7069 (Lynne Ormandy)
Fax: (602) 815-9043
Email: theater@theaterworks.org
Website: www.theaterworks.org

Third Age Theatre Company
Frank Gray
611 East Jackson
Munci, IN 47305
Phone: (765) 288-0822
Email: flgray@bsovc.bsu.edu

Torchbearers
Gloria Weisberg
27 Penny Lane
Cedar Crest, NM 87008
Phone: (505) 286-0413
Email: glo@texoma.net
Sponsor: Santa Fe Playhouse

Touchstone Theatre
Cora Hook
321 E. 4th Street
Bethlehem, PA 18015
Phone: (610) 867-1689 / Fax: (610) 867-0561
Email: touchstone@nni.com

Valley of the Stars Community Theatre
Randall Read
Drawer 1609
Studio City, CA 91611-1609
Phone: (818) 513-7501

Variety Players (Musical group)
Calvert City Office on Aging
450 W. Dares Beach
Prince Frederick, MD 20678

Vintage Players
Ninette S. Mordaunt
8004-C Grand Avenue, N.E.
Albuquerque, NM 87108
Phone: (505) 256-3405
Email: NSmordaunt@juno.com

The Vintage Players
Chuck Burgen
Senior Resource Center, Inc.
252 So. 2nd Street
P.O. Box 506
Frankfort, IN 46041-0506
Phone: (317) 659-4060 or
(317) 659-4440

Vintage Players of Provo Utah
Michael Perry
P.O. Box 692
Orem, UT 84059
Phone: (801) 225-0605
Fax: (801) 765-0489

Young at Heart Chorus
Bob Cilman
Memorial Hall
240 Main Street
Northhampton, MA 01060
Phone: (413) 587-1232

Wrinkles of Washington
Newt Buker
232 N. Rogers
Olympia, WA 98502
Phone: (360) 943-7227

Hamilton City Lights

Rhythm, talent, and vitality are personified in this elite group of dynamic award-winning seniors. Started in 1995, these 59 to 75 year old dancers, known as the *Hamilton City Lights*, brighten every stage on which they perform. Tap, jazz, and musical comedy give them the opportunity to display their energetic, enthusiastic enjoyment of dance.

Hamilton City Lights are featured performers of the annual Golden Age of Variety Show held at the DuMaurier Center every March, and each member, after attending many of Virginia Binko's dance classes, has auditioned to become a part of this dynamic group. Virginia says this was an opportunity "to have an elite group of dancers, to be able to give challenging choreography, to tour, and to increase the awareness of dancing."

The group is available with a presentation of a Broadway revue combining singing, dancing, and comedy where they exude enthusiasm, joy, and a sense of fun to the delight of appreciative audiences. ✰

· · · ·

"These spectacular entertainers are creating an awareness that dance and the performing arts are not just for the young, but also for the young at heart." *Dundas Recorder*

"I love to dance when people are really happy on stage. When you love what you are doing, it spills out into the audience." *Jean, participant*

Hamilton City Lights
Virginia Binko
75 MacNab Street, S.
Hamilton Ontario, Canada L8P 3C1
Phone: (905) 681-2045 (Home)
(905) 529-7727 (Work)
Fax: (905) 522-1820
Sponsor: Hamilton Senior Centre

The Footnotes
Rosemarie Maurice
4089 Lorraine Crescent
Burlington Ontario, Canada L7L 1P5
Phone: (905) 681-1517
Email: tim_maurice@dofasco.ca
(Variety show: Song and Dance
 Throughout the Years)

The Geritol Follies
Chris Hamilton
Hamilton Place
Hamilton Ontario, Canada L0P 4Y3
Phone: (905) 528-8095
Fax: (905) 528-2265
Email: hecfi.com.ca

Raging Grannies of Calgary
Loretta Biasutti
34 Grafton Crescent S.W.
Calgary, Alberta T3E 4X1
Phone: (403) 249-5945
Fax: (403) 249-6917
Email: biasutti@home.com

Raging Grannies of Edmonton
Betty Mardiros
8902 120th Street
Edmonton, Alberta
Canada T6G 1X5
Phone: (780) 439-0445
Email: grannies@compusmart.ab.ca

Raging Grannies of Victoria
Betty Brightwell
855 Wollaston Street
Victoria BC V9A 5A9
Canada
Phone: (250) 383-3130
Email: bbright@pinc.com

(Note: Betty is the editor of The Grapevine, *a newsletter for the many Raging Grannies groups which are in locations around Canada and the U.S.)*

Rhythmic Visions
Rosemarie Maurice
4089 Lorraine Crescent
Burlington Ontario, Canada L7L 1P5
Phone: (905) 681-1517
Email: tim_maurice@dofasco.ca
(Dance classes/workshops for older adults.)

(Dance classes/workshops for older adults.)
Seniors' Jubilee
Glenda Richards
Richburn Entertainment
260 Queen's Quay West, Suite 2805
Toronto Ontario, Canada M5J 2N3
Phone: (416) 260-6755
Fax: (416) 260-5627
Sponsor: Royal Bank

"College, career, marriage, raising a family – all wonderful years of a person's life. But what comes next in one's advancing years? For me, participation in senior theatre has been the opportunity to pick up my childhood love of dancing, music and acting, all under professional guidance. I made new friends who shared similar interests as I showed the world that 'creativity is ageless.' I'll be dancing in the streets at the turn of the century, and at age 85, I'm looking forward to many more years of training and performance in senior theatre."

Dorothy Hake was the choreographer, dance captain, and cheerful participant in the Oregon Senior Theatre and now the Northwest Senior Theatre.

Western Gold Theatre Society

Western Gold Theatre Society, founded in 1994 in Vancouver B.C. by the distinguished Canadian actor Joy Coghill, is a company of professional senior performing artists. The society aims to expand and enrich the lives of senior performers and their audiences. *Western Gold* has produced three major productions including Aaron Bushkowsky's *Strangers Among Us*, a play about the harrowing and sometimes humorous situations that affect both the victims of Alzheimer's Disease and their caregivers, which is soon to go on tour across Canada.

As well as producing full-length stage productions in major theatres, the company, under co-directors Don Mowatt, Anna Hagan, and Pamela Hawthorn, also produces an outreach program of dramatic readings. These are presented at community centers, colleges, and senior facilities taking the message that performers over the age of 55 can play a variety of roles with skill, panache, and insight. ✰

Western Gold Theatre Society

Don Mowatt
1347 Ridgewood Drive
North Vancouver V7R 1J4
B.C. Canada
Phone / Fax: (604) 987-8788
Email: donald_mowatt@bc.sympatico.ca

Victoria Target Theatre Society

An advocate for the elderly for 13 years, *Target Theatre* uses drama as a teaching tool. Performance pieces grow out of requests from health care societies, government ministries, schools, physicians, elder advocates, and others. Each item in the expansive repertoire has been researched and written by *Target* players, and employs various interactive techniques to engage audiences in the learning process. Brochures are available upon request. ☆

• • • •

"Target was fantastic, innovative, and thought provoking. This group should be funded to go to all elder care facilities and should be a pre-requisite for the p.a.c. LPN RN course."

"I wish families could see this one! It might make that difficult situation a little easier."

"A wonderful way to learn improved communication skills in health care situations."

Victoria Target Theatre Society
Yolanda Olivotto
3088 Oakdowne Road
Victoria BC V8R 5N9
Phone: (250) 370-5227
Fax: (250) 598-7199
Email: target@olivottoa.com

PERFORMING GROUPS IN EUROPE & OTHER COUNTRIES

Age Exchange Theatre and Reminiscence Centre

Age Exchange is internationally known for its work in reminiscence, including theatre, publishing, exhibitions, intergenerational projects, and training workshops. *Age Exchange* aims to improve the quality of life of older people by emphasizing the value of their memories through pioneering artistic, educational, and therapeutic activities.

Age Exchange is the only professional reminiscence theatre dedicated to performing plays based on the memories of older people. All of their work emerges from interviews with older people. The material collected is made available to a wider audience through books, exhibitions, and theatre. For 16 years, the organization has been *"Making Memories Matter."*

The Good Companions, *Age Exchange's* senior theatre performing group uses older actors along with professional directors to prepare shows which have been presented to audiences in the UK and across Europe. The group uses Reminiscence Theatre, a life-enhancing method which can help participants revive memories, make new friendships, and build coping skills for difficult life transitions. The group provides entertainment for young and older audiences, encouraging participation in the reminiscence process.

Age Exchange also coordinates the European Reminiscence Network and publishes <u>Reminiscence Magazine</u>, the only professional journal in the field. Several international conferences and festivals exploring leading edge techniques in reminiscence have been conducted over the past few years including, *Remembering Yesterday, Caring Today*, a conference on reminiscence for people with dementia and their family caregivers, held in Vienna in 1998, and *Journey of a Lifetime*, a festival of reminiscence theatre based on the lives of ethnic minority elders, held in London in 1998.

Age Exchange also creates and distributes reminiscence books on themes of social and personal history. Lively and easy to read, they are conversational in style and lavishly illustrated with photographs and drawings of the era.

Based at the Reminiscence Centre, *Age Exchange* also offers a complete schedule of training courses to assist community arts workers, health and social service workers, teachers, and others develop reminiscence groups. The current schedule is available online. ✪

"...these performers were so enjoyable my husband and I plan to see them whenever possible! *Audience member*

"You could tell that all of these wonderful performers give it their all! A thoroughly pleasant experience." *Audience member*

Age Exchange Theatre and Reminiscence Center
Pam Schweitzer
11 Blackheath Village
London England SE3 9LA
Phone: 0181 318 9105
Fax: 0181 318 0060
Email: age-exchange@lewisham.gov.uk
Web: www.age-exchange.org.uk

Aida
Silvia Bevilacqua
Via Pinturicchio, 72
I-06122 Perugia
Italy
Phone/Fax: 0039-75-5727838

Chiedza Theater Group
Ambuya Stella Chiweshe Reich
Stand No. 11788
Kuwadzana Phase 4
PO Mufakose Harare
Zimbabwe
Phone: 00263-11-401885
Email: Chiweshe@africaonline.co.zw

Corporación Colombiana de Teatro
Señora Patricia Ariza
Calle San Miguel de Principe
#12 2-65
Bogota Columbia
Phone: 0057-1-3429621
Fax: 0057-1-2848687

Die Wellenbrecher
Die Wagemutigen
Altentheaterwerkstatt
(Three Theatres)
Angelika Heinich
Landesbühne Niedersachsen Nord
Virchowstrasse 44
D-26382 Wilhelmshaven
Phone: +49(0)4421 940148
Fax: +49(0)4421 940145

The Elements
Lee Gershuny
11 Learmonth Gardens
Edinburgh EH4 1HB, Scotland
Phone: 44-0131-332-1418
Fax: 44-0131-539-9999
Email: 106320.2455@compuserve.com

FestivAge
Monsieur Christian Robert
1 rue Sous le Four
F-63730 Plauzat
France
Phone/Fax: 0033-473-395738

Generationstheater Artemis
Ingrid Türk-Chlapek
A.-Tschabuschnigg-Strasse 12/2
A-9020 Klagenfurt/Celovec
Austria
Phone/Fax: 0043-463-511300

Grupo de Teatro Nucleo 1
Fernanda Coelho
Casa de Cultura, Cx Postal 6001
Cep 86061 Londrina-Parana
Brasil
Phone/Fax: 0055-433248694

Grupo de Terceira Edade
SESC-Londrina Joao Henrique Bernardi
and Alyson Martins Pedrao
B. Fernando de Moronha 264
86020 Londrina, PR
Brasil
Phone: 0055-43-3244949
Fax: 0055-43-3245989

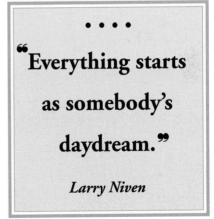

• • • •

"Everything starts

as somebody's

daydream."

Larry Niven

Groupo Fraternidad
Señora Guillermina Fick
calle Julio Condor Flores 453
Coorp. El Augustino Lima
Peru
Phone: 0051-14-3270762
Fax: 0051-14-3272212

Hymittos Theatre
Cleo Mavroudi
39a Parthenonos Street
17562 Palio Falior
Athens, Greece
Phone: 0030 1 983 4328

Impact
Silvain van Labeke
A van Geertstraat 51
9040 Gent
Belgium
Fax: 0032-9238-3485

Kick Théâtre
Monsieur Rene Cheneaux
2, rue Lamertine
F-95240 Cormeilles en Parisis
France
Phone/Fax: 0033-1-34 50 73 37

L'Espace d'un Instant
Dominique Dolmieu
86 Boulevard Diderot
75012 Paris
France
Phone/Fax: 00 33 1 43 40 49 10

Le Volontariat au Service de l'Art
Francoise Vercken
8, rue Miromesnil
F-75008 Paris
France
Phone: 033-1-42666307
Fax: 0033-1-42660554

Okhlopokov Drama Theatre
Anatoly Streltsov
14, Karl.-Marx-Street
664003 Irkutsk
Russia
Phone: 007-3952-241208
Fax: 007-3952-344211

Older People's Drama Group
Centro Comunitario Carcavelos
Av do Loureiro 394
P-2775 Parede
Portugal
Phone: 351 1 457 89 52
Fax: 351 1 457 67 68

Older Women's Network
Maria Teresa Marziali
via del Serraglio 8
I-06073 Corciano PG
Italy
Phone/Fax: 0039-75-5068006

Older Women's Theatre Group
Silvia Bevilacqua
c/o Maria Teresa Marziali
OWN Europe
via del Serraglio 8
06073 Corciano-PG
Perugia
Italy
Phone/Fax: 0039 75 5068006

Older Women's Network & Theatre Group
Ruth Kershaw
34 Greenway Avenue
Thornlie Perth
West Australia 6108
Phone/Fax: 0061-89-4932734

Seniorentheater SeTA e. V
Graf-Recke-Strasse 85
D-40239 Dusseldorf
Germany
Phone: +49(0)211 682600 or 328296

Senior Ensemble of the Freies Werkstatt Theater Köln (Dachverband Altenkultur)

Since 1979, this senior citizen's ensemble, a group of twenty people between the ages of 65 and 83, have been working continuously. In the productions, people's own lives, factors influencing life histories, traditions, and the concept of a personal culture serve as points of departure for improvisation which leads to the development of a play.

The *Dachverband Altenkultur* was organized in 1990 within the framework of an inter-German exchange of experience at the *Freies Werkstatt Theatre Köln* to strengthen self-organization and self-help in the field of senior citizen's culture on an ongoing basis. It was hoped that the work would promote the organizing of cultural activities for senior citizens.

Far removed from any intentions in insulate senior citizens, this umbrella organization wants to represent the interests of older people and bring generations together. Moreover, it promotes communications and attempts to increase senior citizen's awareness of their creative possibilities.

The *Dachverband Altenkultur* has special groups in the areas of theatre, dance/movement, music, storytelling, writing, graphic arts, and work with new media. The umbrella organization is active throughout Germany, is interdisciplinary and intergenerational. With its inter-topical approach, it seeks to take artistic and social aspects equally into account, building bridges in many ways.

For example:
- Cooperation between agencies organizing cultural opportunities for senior citizens;
- Communication of experience;
- Gathering and disseminating information;
- Publishing an information service (i.e., *Das Forum des Dachverbandes Alktenkultur*);
- Organizing conferences; and
- Consulting with agencies working on model projects.

In January 1992, work was begun to establish a second office in Leipzig. An Office for Senior Citizens' Culture has been working there since April 1993. In addition to a complex program of continuing education, the staff offers guidance to senior citizens in all areas of art to promote their creative involvement. ✩

Dachverband Altenkultur
Freies Werkstatt Theater Köln
Dieter Scholz and Ingrid Berzau
Zugweg 10
D-50677 Köln
Germany
Phone: +49(0)221-327817 or 323502
Fax: +49(0)221-331668 / Email: Uwfev@aol.com

Seniorentheater Spätlese e. V

Günter Kingner
Haus der Kunste
Lindenstrasse 6
D-1230 Frankfurt (Oder)
Germany
Phone: +40(0)335 326284

Snippets Historical and Cultural Drama Group

Phil O'Regan
19 Ashleigh Drive
Skehard Road
Cork, Ireland
Phone/Fax: 00353-21-294336

Stut Theater

Frau Ingeborg Hornsveld
Lange Lauwerstraat 69
NL-3512 VH Utrecht
Holland
Phone: 0031-30-2311801 / Fax: 0031-30-2311427

Tanztheater Dritter Frühling

Charlotte Madörin
Bauherrenstr. 43
CH-8049 Zürich
Switzerland
Phone/Fax: 0041-1-3416558

Theater Alt and Jung

Frank Matzke
Specke 12
31139 Hildesheim
Germany
Phone/Fax: 0049 5121 62381

Theater der Erfahrungen

Eva Bittner and Johanna Kaiser
Nachbarschaftsheim Berlin Schöneberg
Cranachstrasse 52
D-12157 Berlin
Germany
Phone: 0049-303-8554206
Fax: 0049-303-8554378

Theater Mühleimer Spatlese

Eckhard Friedl
Kulturamt der Stadt Mühlheim a.d. Ruhr
Leineweberstrasse 1
D-45466 Mühlheim a.d. Ruhr
Phone: 0049-208-4554119
Fax: 0049-208-4554199

Theatergroep Delta

Mr. Marcel van Kempen
Korte Leidsewarsstraat 12
NL-1017 RC Amsterdam
Holland
Phone: 0031626-20-1435
Fax: 0031-20-4210639

Teatr Osrodek Stacja Szamocin

Frau Luba Zarembinska
Ul. Dworcowa 17A
P1-64-820-Szamocin
Poland
Phone: 0048-67-2848114
Fax: 0048-67-2848895

Uhan Shii Theatre

Ms. Ya-Ling Peng
Fl.2, No. 97. Der Shin West Rd., 111
Taipei, Taiwan
Phone: 00886-2-8866 1116
Fax: 00886-2-8866 1954

Universita III Etá

Nicoletta Robello (CSRT)
Via Manzoni 22
I-50025 Pontedera (Pisa)
Italy
Phone: 0039-587-55720
Fax: 0039-587-213631

Werk-en Studiengroep

Keative Dans voor Ouderen Sima van Dullenmen
Deltastraat 14 (1)
NL-1078 PC Amsterdam
Holland
Phone: 0031-20-6738440

PERFORMING ARTISTS
& PRESENTING ORGANIZATIONS

PERFORMING ARTISTS

Barbara O. Korner

Barbara holds a Ph.D. in interdisciplinary fine arts from Ohio University and has an M.A. in Oral Interpretation and a B.S. in Directing. She has served on the theatre faculty of the University of Missouri-Columbia, Ohio University and Seattle Pacific University, where she was the Dean of Fine and Performing Arts. She is the coeditor with Carla Waal of *Hardship and Hope: Missouri Women Writing About Their Lives, 1820-1920*, an anthology based on their two-woman show about pioneering Missouri women. ☆

Her Performances:

Responding to the Call:
Women of Spiritual Action

Using the writings of 19th century African-American women preachers, this program explores the themes of the appeal of Methodism to African-American women, the influence of African-American religion on American worship, and the sense of power and autonomy possessed by women preachers.

Questions of Identity: Creating Sacred Spaces

Using the writings of women from a variety of cultural backgrounds, the central theme of this program is the restorative power of women's exploration of the spiritual and sacred in a rapidly fragmenting society.

Barbara O. Korner
9906 242nd Place, S.W.
Edmonds, WA 98020
Phone: (206) 542-8975
Email: bkorner@cmc.net

PERFORMING ARTISTS *(Continued)*

Kathryn E. Smith as Elizabeth Barrett Browning.

Kathryn E. Smith

Actress, director, costumer and writer, Kathryn has been working in the theatre for decades as both an amateur and as a professional. Her credits include theatres from Baltimore, Maryland to Tokyo, Japan, where she studied Oriental theatre.

Her one-woman shows have been well received by schools, womens' organizations, such as the Daughters of the American Revolution, the Homemakers, as well as numerous senior audiences.

Her Performances:

The Presidents' Ladies and Mistress Maryland

These collections of short vignettes portray the lives of eight of our presidents' wives and ten famous women of Maryland, including Martha Washington, Mary Todd Lincoln, Eleanor Roosevelt, Margaret Brent, Rosa Ponselle, and Harriet Tubman.

Women - Thy Name is Diversity

This performance creates a full woman by selecting specific character traits from women in theatre, music, and poetry, including Cho-Cho-San, Carmen, Clytaemnestra, Dolly Levi, An Inventor's Wife, Madame Arcati, and others.

All of the programs use props and costumes to enhance the visual effect. ✩

Kathryn E. Smith
196 Fulbright Court
Severna Park, MD 21146-3218
Phone: (410) 647-1843
Email: KENKATHRYN1@prodigy.net

Al Cherry
1717 Woodwell Road
Silver Springs, MD 20906
Phone: (301) 460-3620

PRESENTING ORGANIZATIONS

Hospital Audiences, Inc.

The goals of *HAI* are to provide access to the arts for people who are isolated from the cultural mainstream in the New York City area. The organization either brings audiences to sites of visual and performing arts experiences or presents the arts directly to them on-site in institutions. *HAI* also uses the arts to convey lifesaving information about critical public health issues to improve the decision making skills of the participants. ☆

Hospital Audiences, Inc.
Michael Jon Spencer
548 Broadway, 3rd Floor
New York, NY 10012-3912
Phone: (212) 575-7676
Fax: (212) 575-7669
Email: hospaud@aol.com
Website: www.hospitalaudiences.org

National Theatre Community Vaudeville

The *National's Vaudeville* program, begun in 1995, sends entertainers to hospitals, senior centers, and retirement residences in the Greater Washington D.C. area. Performances by musicians, singers, poets, dancers, and magicians are free to nonprofit locales. ☆

National Theatre Community Vaudeville
Executive Offices
1321 Pennsylvania Avenue, N.W.
Washington, D.C. 20004
No phone calls please.
Email: dbm@nationaltheatre.org
Website: www.nationaltheatre.org

• • • •

"Bridging the gap that exists after retirement from regular work was made easier by joining a senior theatre group and participating wholeheartedly with enthusiasm and commitment. The fellowship it engendered created an ongoing and very satisfying personal experience. Being in the *Oregon Senior Theatre* was wonderful and successful — full of pleasure, fun, and a feeling of accomplishment."

Ed Seibert has been a lifelong theatre lover who, when he retired, joined a play viewing group and later the Oregon Senior Theatre appearing as a singer, actor, and joke-teller extraordinaire!

Charles J. Ault
Player's Guild of the Festival Playhouse
P.O. Box 944
Arvada, CO 80001-0944
Phone: (303) 422-4090
Fax: (303) 421-5404

Wendell Barnes
Arts for All
57 Forsyth Street, N.W., Ste. R-1
Atlanta, GA 30303
Phone: (404) 221-1270, ext. 20
Fax: (404) 221-1984
Tty: (404) 221-2537
Email: artsforall@mindspring.com
Website: www.atlantacares.com

Dr. Ann Davis Basting
Interactive, Intergenerational Storytelling Project
  Center for 20th Century Studies,
University of Wisconsin Milwaukee
P.O. Box 413
Milwaukee, WI 53201
Phone: (414) 229-5961
Fax: (414) 229-5964
Email: Basting@uwm.edu

Dr. Victoria Coffman
Professor of Theatre
Montana State University
Billings, MT 59101-0298
Phone: (406) 657-2178
Fax: (406) 657-2187

Lillian Misko-Coury
Penn State University Continuing Ed.
New Kensington Campus
3550 7th Street. RD. Route 780
New Kensington, PA 15068
Phone: (724) 334-6716
Fax: (724) 334-6116
Email: lmc1@psu.edu

Thomas V. Gaydos
6516 Banner Lake Circle #5107
Orlando, FL 32821-7303

M. Charline Gowen
The Imagination Power Company
5245 Columbia Road
Evans, GA 30809
Phone: (706) 863-5918
Email: impowerco@aol.com

Dawn Lane
326 Old Stockbridge Road
Lenox, MA 01240
Phone: (413) 637-0230
Email: Dawnlane40@aol.com

Liz Lerman
7117 Maple Avenue
Takoma Park, MD 20912
Phone: (301) 270-6700 / Fax: (301) 270-2626
Email: artsource@compuserve.com

Don Loeffler
2705 West Cluster Avenue
Tampa, FL 33614-4367
Phone: (813) 931-3458
Fax: (813) 933-5238
Email: dllcfm@gte.net

Dr. Ann McDonough
University of Nevada Las Vegas
4505 S. Maryland Parkway
Las Vegas, NV 89154-5036
Phone: (702) 895-4248 / Fax: (702) 895-0833
Email: mdonoua@nevada.edu

Steven Pennell
SPRI Theatre Company
Brown University
Box 1148
Providence, RI 02912
Phone: (401) 863-1815
Fax: (401) 863-3559

Annette Cantrell Epstein

("A Theatre Productions Agency - All In One Person!")
From its inception, Annette has been part of *Senior Follies*, a senior theatre organization from Anderson, South Carolina, which is celebrating ten wonderfully successful and profitable years of first-class, semiprofessional entertainment. Annette produces, writes, composes, directs, choreographs, records instrumental tracks, and plays the accompaniment for *Senior Follies*. She is the first, however, to give credit to the tremendously talented people who participate in the *Follies* and all of the wisdom they bring to the organization.

"I believe *Senior Follies* is successful for several reasons. First, as a director, the more positive energy I can pour into a group, the more I get back. The cast is overflowing with creative enthusiasm and positive spirit! Secondly, the people have all kinds of untapped talent and they eagerly await the opportunity to share their gifts. Most importantly, it is my philosophy that everyone in senior theatre is a star and deserves the opportunity to be front and center sometime during a show."

Senior Follies has become one of the most highly anticipated productions in upstate South Carolina. Each year, original shows are written so every performance is new and refreshing for both the performers and the audience. "As a director, I believe every rehearsal should spark energy and enthusiasm, and if I can light a fire in a cast member on stage, pretty soon the entire theater is blazing with astounding color and life!"

"I can honestly say that our organization is the exception to every rule. We make a profit of thousands of dollars each year, we have rehearsal and performance space, as well as a collection of hundreds of costumes, and a place to store them! We have a technical crew and ideas beyond belief, and above all, WE HAVE FUN!" Call Annette to help you or your organization! ☆

Annette Cantrell Epstein
2907 Rambling Path
Anderson, SC 29621
Phone: (864) 226-8810
Fax: (864) 226-4799
Email: epstein@carol.net

Joy Reilly

During her fifteen years as Founding Artistic Director of *Grandparents Living Theatre*, Reilly wrote and directed eight scripts for the company, including the Emmy award winning "*I Was Young, Now I'm Wonderful!*" Highlights of her GLT leadership include representing the USA with "*...Wonderful!*" at the 1991 International Conference in Cologne, Germany, headlining at the 1994 National Council on Aging Annual Convention in Washington DC., residencies in schools and colleges, appearing on the BBC, ABC, CNN, and PBS, directing "*GLT doing Pinter*" at the International Pinter Festival, and sponsoring the first residency in Columbus of a Russian theatre company of distinguished older artists. Reilly's work was subsidized by the Ohio Arts Council, corporations, foundations, medical associations, hospitals, and gerontology programs.

In October 1997, Reilly served as a visiting artist at UNLV's playwrighting program. She has taught workshops throughout the United States and overseas and works with all age groups, specializing in creative writing out of oral history. In March 1998, Reilly resigned from GLT to have more time to create new work. Now she teaches, directs, writes, and acts as well as advises on theses and dissertations. She recently wrote and directed a new intergenerational farce about the afterlife titled "*I've Almost Got the Hang of It!*" for GLT with guest OSU undergraduates.

Joy Reilly, Ph.D., Ohio State University Theatre Professor, specializes in creating and directing new work with older actors.

Among all of her many talents, she can also serve as a workshop leader, guest artist, consultant and director, and can help you create new work. Contact her to find out about Ohio State University's new Interdisciplinary Aging Specialty. ✩

Contact Joy to obtain more information about her original scripts:
"*I Was Young, Now I'm Wonderful!*" (6m.6f) musical
"*A Picket Fence, Two Kids, and a Dog Named Spot!*" (4m, 4f) musical
"*Sappho's Women*" (9f)
"*Golden Age is all the Rage*" (12-16 actors)
"*I've Almost Got the Hang of It!*" (4m, 5f) musical

Joy Reilly
Department of Theatre
Ohio State University
Columbus, OH 43220
Phone (Office): (614) 292-0804 or
  (614) 457-5765
Fax: (614) 457-0148
Email: reilly.3@osu.edu

Susan Perlstein
Elders Share the Arts
72 East First Street
New York, NY 10003
Phone: (212) 780-1928
Fax: (212) 529-5062
Email: elderarts@aol.com

Ruth S. Pierce
5201 Chandler Street
Bethesda, MD 20814
Phone: (301) 897-5987
Email: fran-ruth-pierce@worldnet.att.net

Paula Rais
Mass. Cultural Council Elder Arts Initiative
120 Boylston Street
Boston, MA 02116
Phone: (617) 727-3668
Fax: (617) 423-0580
Email: prais53@aol.com

Olivia Raynor, Ph.D., OTR
c/o National Arts and Disability Center
300 UCLA Medical Plaza, Ste. 330
Box 956967
Los Angeles, CA 90095-6967
Fax: (310) 794-1143
Email: oraynor@mednet.ucla.edu
Webside: www.npi.ucla.edu/ata

Dana Singer
Business of Writing for the Theatre
2275 Amigo Drive
Missoula, MT 59802
Phone: (406) 728-5248
Fax: (406) 728-2729

Doug Stewart
One Cerrado Court
Santa Fe, NM 87505
Phone / Fax: (505) 466-4724
Email: Stewart@rt66.com

Lois Stienike
Grand Generation Center
304 E. 3rd
P.O. Box 1302
Grand Island, NE 68801
Phone: (308) 385-5308
Fax: (308) 385-5312

Paula Terry
Coordinator of Office for AccessAbility
National Endowment for the Arts
1100 Pennsylvania Ave., N.W.
Washington, D.C. 20506
Phone: (202) 682-5530
Email: terryp@arts.endow.gov

Bonnie L. Vorenberg
Senior Theatre Connections
ArtAge Publications
P.O. Box 12271
Portland, OR 97212-0271
Phone / Fax: (503) 249-1137
Email: bonniev@teleport.com
Website: http://www.seniortheatre.com

Naida D. Weisberg
!Improvise! Inc.
Box 2473
Providence, RI 02906
Phone: (401) 274-3418 or
   (401) 272-0226

Rosilyn Wilder, Ed.D., RDT/DCT
10 Clairidge Court
Montclair, NJ 07042
(Phone: (973) 746-5184
Email: RozWilder@aol.com

Sarah Worthington
Footsteps of the Elders
693 Yaronia Drive
Columbus, OH 43214
Phone: (614) 262-2033
Fax: (614) 890-5220
Email: carter.3@osu.edu

PUBLISHERS, PLAYWRIGHTS, & SCRIPTS

*P*laywrights have found senior theatre and they are loving it! Many have emerged out of necessity–their performing group needs a script, so they write one. But the thrill of seeing their words on stage is captivating and suddenly they find themselves both entranced and prolific. Interestingly, many of the playwrights are seniors using drama to convey their thoughts about aging with insight and humor. Some are studying at academic programs such as *University of Nevada Las Vegas (UNLV)* where playwrighting is a major thrust. Other organizations, such as *Playwrights Anonymous*, have emerged with a primary purpose of promoting playwrights for senior theatre. Whatever their age or purpose, the writers are busily working at writing and getting their work produced.

And the writers are having success, an obvious fact from the many publishers who feature plays for senior performers. Of course, all welcome submissions.

Scripts with characters that speak about aging in new voices are necessary to meet the upcoming growth in the field. All types of plays–from short comedies to longer dramas to variety shows, will be in demand to accommodate the new generation of seniors wanting to be heard.

Our hope is that *Senior Theatre Connections* will help bring aspiring playwrights into contact with performing groups to refine the scripts and then with publishers to distribute them. ✰

Adamson, Jo J. (Playwright)
25252 Lake Wilderness
Country Club Drive, S.E.
Maple Valley, WA 98038
Phone: (425) 432-0823
Fax: (425) 413-2639
Email: jowrite@email.msn.com

Armory Square Playhouse (Playwright/ Producer)
David Feldman, Artistic Director
1062 Westmoreland Avenue
Syracuse, NY 13210
Phone: (315) 426-9149
Email: feldmand@aurora.sunyocc.edu

Anchorage Press, Inc. (Publisher)
O.R. Corey
P.O. Box 8067
New Orleans, LA 70182
Phone: (504) 283-8868
Fax: (504) 866-0502

Austin Scriptworks (Playwright's Group)
P. Paullette MacDougal
4115 Firstview Drive
Austin, TX 78731
Fax: (512) 452-5101
Email: PMFM@aol.com

Baker's Plays (Publisher)
100 Chauncy Street
Boston, MA 02111
Phone: (617) 482-1280
Fax: (617) 482-7614
Website: www.bakersplays.com

Bill Benton(Playwright)
516 Ponderosa Drive
Fort Collins, CO 80521-3133
Phone: (970) 224-5326
Fax: (970) 416-8885
Email: wmbenton@earthlink.net

Bi-Folkal Productions (Publisher)

Chuckle over large-print scripts for 20 humorous short skits in *Almost Anything for a Laugh*. Each skit is designed to prompt memories, discussion, and laughter. Multiple copies are three-hole punched in a ring binder, easy to use, store, and use again. Production notes on sets, props, and presentation techniques are included. Order SK 395 $25. Multiple copies of 10 or more skits can be found in *Anything for a Laugh, Too!* Order SK 397 $15. ($5 S/H per order).

Bi-Folkal Productions is a nonprofit corporation organized in 1976 to encourage reminiscence and the sharing of experiences between generations, weaving the past into the future. Break a leg–and the ice, too!

Here is a sample of the large print from *Fun and Games with Grandma*:

Grandma: It's a *thimble*. It's used for hand sewing.
Grandchild: Why would *anyone* want to sew their hand?! ✩

Bi-Folkal Productions, Inc.
Lynne Martin Erickson
809 Williamson
Madison, WI 53703
Phone: (608) 251-2818
Orders: (800) 568-5357
Fax: (608) 251-2874
Email: bifolks@globaldialog.com

When Is The Train Due? From <u>Remembering Train Rides</u>.

Kimberly Chin (Playwright)

c/o John Chin
2245 Peach Avenue, #4
Clovis, CA 93612
Phone: (702) 650-5393 (Home)
John: (209) 294-1638
Email: kimchin@nevada.edu

Harold Cohen (Playwright/Publisher)

135 Atlantic Place
Hauppauge, NY 11788
Phone: (516) 234-9379

I.E. Clark Publications (Publisher)

P.O. Box 246
Schulenburg, TX 78956-0246
Phone: (409) 743-3232
Fax: (409) 743-4765
Email: ieclark@cvtv.net

Dramatic Publishing (Publisher)

311 Washington Street
Woodstock, IL 60098
Phone: (800) 448-7469
Fax: (800) 334-5302
Website: www.dramaticpublishing.com

Your place for resources for the mature actor!

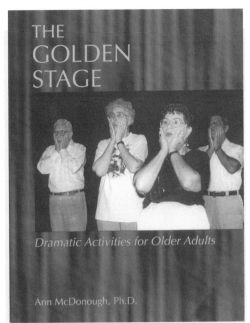

The Golden Stage:
Dramatic Activities for Older Adults

By Ann McDonough.
Make an entrance into *The Golden Stage*, a text which introduces senior adults to the art and craft of acting. This practical handbook by senior adult theatre expert Ann McDonough includes a variety of theatre games and exercises in managing stage fright, concentration, relaxation and memorization. Approaches to preparing for auditions, analyzing characters and performing scenes are also incorporated, along with practical suggestions for creating both musical and oral history revues. *8 ½ by 11 with 283 pages.* Well illustrated with photographs and drawings.
Price $23.95   *Code: G 62*

The Golden Stage:
Teacher's Guide

By Ann McDonough.
The Golden Stage: Teacher's Guide is the instructor's companion piece for the text above and provides a step-by-step process for using the text in senior acting classes. Practical information on the physical and social conditions of older adults, recruiting students and adapting to the special needs and interests of older adults is included. This is a very helpful book for professionals who wish either to start a senior theatre program or to teach classes. *8 ½ by 11 with 86 pages.*
Price $12.95   *Code: G 99*

New Monologues for Mature Actors

Compiled and edited by Ann McDonough.
This first-of-its-kind anthology of comic and serious monologues is specially tailored for actors age 55 and older. Leading American playwrights have penned characters who are fresh and reflective of older adults in the modern world. A convenient sourcebook of monologues ideally suited for auditions or acting classes, the book also contains suggestions and exercises to use when preparing for an audition, plus listings of previously published and produced classical, comic and serious monologues for mature actors and actresses. A must for senior performers! *9 x 6 with 190 pages.*
Price $19.95   *Code: N44*

Short Stuff: Ten- to Twenty-Minute Plays for Mature Actors

Edited by Ann McDonough.
This new anthology of short plays offers a wide variety of challenging roles for actors over the age of 55. *Short Stuff* dramatizes the lives of distinctive and memorable characters: Harriet, a sixty-some-thing dynamo who returns to college to earn her degree; Georgie and Sass who discover the power of laughter and acceptance in the face of adversity; Howard and Ellie who endure a stormy blind date arranged through a dating service; Edwin and Phyllis whose marriage survives the existence of Edwin's diary of women; and Dick and Rusty who play out a romantic gun-totin' fantasy of the Old West. And more: Mr. Ponazecki who laments the passing of a favorite hotel; a cleaning lady who feels like a queen when she steps into the shoes of a beauty pageant contestant; two sisters who come to terms with a husband's infidelity; a derelict and his relationship with a woman seeking the warmth of companionship; and two friends who learn that friendship is far more valuable than winning a jackpot. *9x6 with 269 pages.*
Price $19.95   *Code: SC8*

New Plays for Mature Actors

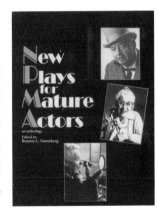

Anthology. Edited by Bonnie L. Vorenberg.
"A decidedly unique collection... The 10 plays and sketches provide opportunities for seniors to utilize their skills as actors... The plays' plots and characters put forth, by design, a positive image of the aging experience." (*Booklist*, American Library Association) Edited by the artistic director of the Oregon Senior Theatre Ensemble, *New Plays for Mature Actors* "will be an excellent resource for individuals and groups who sense the stirring of their creative energy in later life and turn to the theatre for its expression." (Priscilla McCutcheon, National Center on Arts and the Aging) *New Plays for Mature Actors* is typeset in extra-large type to make it exceptionally readable and widely accessible to readers with limited vision. *8 ½ x 11 with 187 pages.*
Price $19.95   *Code: N38*

Acting Up!

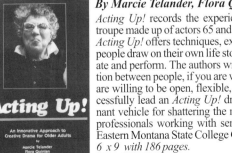

By Marcie Telander, Flora Quinlan, and Karol Verson.
Acting Up! records the experiences of a touring improvisational theatre troupe made up of actors 65 and older. Using humor and outspoken honesty, *Acting Up!* offers techniques, exercises and sketches aimed at helping older people draw on their own life stories as they learn to express themselves, create and perform. The authors write: "If you care about quality communication between people, if you are willing to take a risk in order to create, if you are willing to be open, flexible, vulnerable and experimental, you can successfully lead an *Acting Up!* drama group." "*Acting Up!* provides a poignant vehicle for shattering the myths of ageism. It is a must for all theatre professionals working with senior adults," writes Victoria Tait Coffman, Eastern Montana State College Gerontology Center.
6 x 9 with 186 pages.
Price $16.95   *Code: A58*

Dramatic Publishing

Phone: 800-448-7469 Fax: 800-334-5302
311 Washington Street, Woodstock, IL 60098 USA *Visa and Master Card accepted.*
Visit our website at: www.dramaticpublishing.com Ask for our free catalog which features many plays suitable for the mature actor.

Encore Performance Publishing (Publisher)

Mike Perry
P.O. Box 692
Orem, UT 84059
Phone: (801) 225-0605
Fax: (801) 765-0489
Email: Encoreplay@aol.com
Website: www.encoreplay.com

Annette Cantrell Epstein (Playwright)

2907 Rambling Path
Anderson, SC 29621
Phone: (864) 226-8810
Fax: (864) 226-4799
Email: epstein@carol.net

Joseph J. Finnerty (Playwright)

8207 E. Horseshoe Lane
Scottsdale, AZ 85250
Phone: (602) 948-9972
Fax: (602) 951-8424
Email: finnertyjj@aol.com

Jim Gustafson (Playwright)

1280 Windsor Drive
Wheaton, IL 60187
Phone: (630) 668-9356
Fax: (630) 668-3134
Email: derfdugan@aol.com

❧ ENCORE PERFORMANCE PUBLISHING ❧

Encore Performance Publishing is a young and growing publisher of plays, musicals and short plays for amateur, educational and professional theatre groups. We specialize in family-oriented material. Plays about family life are strongly encouraged. We have plays that are perfect for groups whose primary audience enjoys "G" and "PG" rated material. We have a large stock of plays for teen and child audiences and a growing number of plays focusing on "Seniors" in theatre.

Our plays are meant to uplift and entertain, promote self-worth, healthy life-styles and encourage upright social behavior. However, our plays don't preach! They have a message or a theme supporting the goals of our company, but they are not didactically involved in presenting their message.

A few of our Senior Theatre titles are:

> **Ladies at Lunch**, by Carol Woods
> **Ladies at Poker**, by Carol Woods
> **Ladies on Vacation**, by Carol Woods
> **Listen to the Snow**, by Max C. Golightly
> **String of Lights**, by Terry Earp
> **Green Bough in My Heart**, by Ruth and Nathan Hale
> **Journey to the Big Sky**, by Jack Weyland
> **You're Never Too...**, by Brenda Sinclair

There are many other titles that include Senior Actors and Actresses in the cast.

Encore Performance Publishing
P.O. Box 692
Orem, UT 84059
Phone: (801) 225-0605 / Fax: (801) 765-0489
Email: Encoreplay@aol.com / Website: www.Encoreplay.com

SENIOR THEATRE SCRIPTS
by Vern Harden
Audience Tested and Approved!

"Seasoned Citizens"

Few shows feature a dead man who cheats at checkers and argues with the doctor about his own death! Yet, Zelda wants to marry him and have fourteen children! This proven laugh-getter features unique characters, is simple to produce, and has actor-proof lines. 'Citizens' is a classic!

"Boardinghouse"

Features the world's worst poet, a cash-and-carry psychic and a hypochondriac who is certain her nose is going to fall off. Then, Dirk Shadows arrives to lead the search for buried gold. A hilarious, easy to produce mystery/comedy. Audience tested and approved!

"Don't Drop Momma!"

An overprotective daughter, scandal hungry friends and an aging Romeo can turn any world upside down! When two people end up stuck in the same chair, the word spreads and...!!! You have the funniest new show in years!

"Lettuce Honey, You're Quite a Dish! or Can a wood, Chuck Save Me Now?"

A two-act melodrama that's more fun than a barrel of monkeys! Featuring two villains (one has trouble kneeling to propose), two heroines (one is hard of hearing), and the ever bumbling hero, Chuck Wood. For more information on these and other Senior Theatre scripts, write:

Vern Harden
(Playwright/Publisher)
Box 78
Cedaredge, CO 81413
Phone: (970) 856-7430
Fax: (970) 856-3577
Email: v_m_harden@hotmail.com

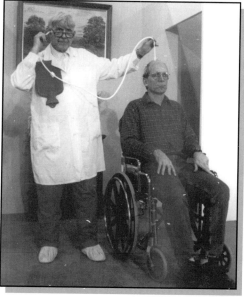

Scene from "Seasoned Citizens."

Werner Hashagen (Playwright)
5645 Rutgers Road
La Jolla, CA 92037-7827
Phone: (619) 459-0122
Email: wrh@inetworld.net
Website: www.inetworld.net/wrh

**Heart of the Matter Productions
(Playwright)**
Cathy Plourade
RR1 Box 1271
Springvale, ME 04083
Phone: (207) 324-4074

Norbert Hruby (Playwright)
245 Briarwood, SE
Grand Rapids, MI 49506
Phone: (616) 459-1149
Email: norbdolor@worldnet.att.net

Daphne R. Hull (Playwright)
841 Park Avenue
Baltimore, MD 21201
Phone: (410) 783-5729
Email: ink@ix.netcom.com
Website: www.cwave.com/users/sdempsey/hull.htm

James & Bronwyn Jameson (Playwrights)
32564 Captain's Galley
Avon Lake, OH 44012
Phone: (440) 933-3960
Fax: (440) 930-3727
Email: jameson@mediawave.com

Carleen Jaspers (Playwright)
P.O. Box 71184
Las Vegas, NV 89170
Phone: (702) 791-5197 or
   (702) 263-3630
Email: jaspers@nevada.edu

Gerry Lekas (Playwright)
621 Long Road
Glenview, IL 60025
Phone: (847) 729-2856
Email: GLekas007@aol.com

Terryl Paiste (Playwright/Publisher)
4249 Berritt Street
Fairfax, VA 22030-3546
Phone: (703) 273-1047
Fax: (703) 273-2046
Email: GPaiste@prodigy.com

Pioneer Drama Service (Publisher)
P.O. Box 4267
Englewood, CO 80155
Phone: (800) 333-7262 / (303) 779-4035
Fax: (303) 779-4315
Email: piodrama@aol.com
Website: www.pioneerdrama.com

Playwrights Anonymous (Support Group)

Playwrights Anonymous is a support group for Washington D.C. area dramatists caught "in the visious web of playwrighting addiction." Their plays for seniors have been published in many anthologies, most recently *Short Stuff: Ten to Twenty Minute Plays for Mature Actors*. Senior theatres that have produced their works include Cupertino Senior Center, Griswold Senior Center, Masque Club of Greenbriar, Royal Highlands, Seniors Reaching Out, Vintage Players, and others. They welcome inquiries from senior theatres looking for anything from short monologues to full-length plays for mature actors. ☆

Playwrights Anonymous
Terryl Paiste
4249 Berritt Street
Fairfax, VA 22030-3546
Phone: (703) 273-1047
Fax: (703) 273-2046
Email: GPaiste@prodigy.com

Pleasant Hill Press (Publisher)
Ted Fuller
241 Greenwich Drive
Pleasant Hill, CA 94523
Phone: (925) 932-2049
Fax: (925) 932-2049 (call first)
Email: TedPress@aol.com
Website: http://members.aol.com/tedpress/
   index.html

Popular Play Service (Publisher)
Janet H. Dow
P.O. Box 1206
Woodbury, CT 06798
Phone: (203) 263-2546
Fax: (203) 263-6232

Readers Theatre Script Service (Publisher)
P.O. Box 178333
San Diego, CA 92177
Phone / Fax: (619) 576-7369

Return Engagement Plays (Publisher)
Jules Abrams
2720 Blaine Drive
Chevy Chase, MD 20815-3042
Phone / Fax: (301) 585-9689
Email: jules368@juno.com

Stage & Screen Book Club (Publisher)
P6550 East 30th Street
P.O. Box 6372
Indianapolis, IN 46206-6372
Website: www.StageNScreen.com

Beth Campell Stemple (Playwright)
This Wide & Universal Theatre
P.O. Box 665
Mystic, CT 06355-0665
Phone: (860) 599-2857
Email: bstemple@uconect.net
Website: http://hot.uconect.net/-bstemple/
   main.htm

More plays for senior theatre can be found in the Bibliography under the "Play Anthologies" heading.

PIONEER DRAMA HAS THE BEST PLAYS FOR SENIORS

Admissions

And the Fullness Thereof

Child of Air

Ho, Ho Tyranny!

It Hardly Matters Now

Lovesong

Miss Twiddle and the Devil

The Mouse and the Raven

Mystery Guest

Not Far from the Giaconda Tree

Not My Cup of Tea

A Plane to Somewhere

Spirit!

You Can't Be Too Careful

plus a wide selection of melodramas

Call today for a free copy of our catalog

1-800-333-7262

Phone: 303-779-4035 • **Fax:** 303-779-4315
E-Mail: piodrama@aol.com
Website: www.pioneerdrama.com
Address: P.O. Box 4267 • Englewood, Colorado 80155

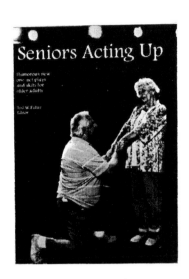
• • • •

Senior theatre performers are extroverts—people who are content to be themselves without apology. I call them 'characters'. We are colorful, interesting, and usually have a sense of humor that makes it easy for us to laugh at ourselves, even on stage. We were all born to do what we do—sing, dance, act, make people laugh—but there's more!

Over the years, a bonding developed among performers. We have become a second family to each other. As tired and weary as we sometimes get from nine months of rehearsals and shows, we still return every Fall, with very few exceptions, to start all over again.

I admit to feelings of guilt when I am asked to spend my time helping in other directions, but I was healed by an eight year-old boy who came to me after a show in Klamath Falls. With his eyes sparkling and a big smile on his face, he said, "Before I saw your show I was afraid of growing old, but now I'm not afraid anymore." That alone made it all worthwhile. We make a difference!

Jean Rose, performer for 12 years with the Oregon Senior Theatre and the Northwest Senior Theatre.

    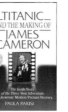  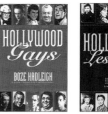 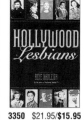

0117 $30.00/**$19.95**   0943 $19.95/**$9.95**   1008   **$9.99x**   0760   **$12.95x***   0893 $24.95/**$14.95***   1172   **$13.95x**   0422 $21.95/**$15.95**   3350 $21.95/**$15.95**

3368 $14.95/**$11.95**   3376 $19.95/**$15.95**   3384 $22.50/**$18.00**

0927-9999# $40.00/**$29.95**

   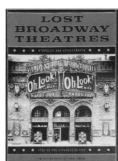

3392 $24.95/**$17.50**   3418 $19.95/**$15.95**   3426 $10.95/**$9.00**

3400-9999# $24.95/**$21.50**

    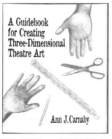

0067 $14.95/**$11.95+**   3442 $15.00/**$11.00**   1578 $17.95/**$14.95+**

2121 $19.95/**$15.95+**   3111 $16.95/**$13.50+**   3129 $19.95/**$15.95+**   3434-9999# $26.95/**$19.95**

3087 $19.95/**$15.95+**   1016 $25.00/**$14.95**   0414 $10.95/**$8.95*+**   2857 $12.99/**$9.99+**   1065 $21.95/**$13.20**   1081 $23.95/**$18.95**   0208 $25.95/**$15.50***   0810   **$9.99x**

5 REASONS TO JOIN NOW

1. Joining is easy. Start with 4 books for $1. Your bill (including shipping and handling) will come when membership is confirmed. **2. Your satisfaction is guaranteed.** If you're not happy with your 4 books, return them within 10 days *at our expense.* Your membership will be canceled; you'll owe nothing. **3. Save up to 50% off publishers' hardcover edition prices.** Every book we offer is a high-quality, full-text edition, sometimes altered in size to fit special presses. Just pick at least 4 more books at our regular low prices during your membership. Take up to 2 years! Then you may resign any time. **4. A FREE Club Magazine** comes to you up to 17 times a year—plus up to 2 special issues. Each reviews the Featured Book Selections plus dozens of alternate books. Some are exclusive Club editions you won't find anywhere else. **5. Ordering is risk-free.** Featured Book Selections are sent to you automatically. To cancel—or order other books—simply mail in your Member Reply Form by the marked date. As a member, you can also order books via our Web site **(www.StageNScreen.com)**. Shipping and handling (plus sales tax, where applicable) is added to each order. You'll always have 10 days to decide. If your Member Reply Form is late and unwanted books arrive, please return them *at our expense.*

Prices shown were current at press time.
Prices in fine print are for publishers' editions.
Prices in bold print are for Club editions.

D945

 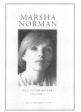 

NEED HELP GETTING THE WORD OUT?

ArtAge Publications can help you expand your marketing by:

- Marketing consultations

- Creating web pages

- Mailing lists available for senior theatre

Capitalize on the many resources we have found in senior theatre. Thorough and complete, we can help you reach our very unique market. Call on us at:

ArtAge Publications
P.O. Box 12271
Portland, OR 97212-0271
(503) 249-1137
Email: bonniev@teleport.com
Website: www.seniortheatre.com

When you want to reach everyone in
senior theatre,
turn to ArtAge Publications!

OTHER OPPORTUNITIES IN SENIOR THEATRE

**Academic Programs
Acting in Commercials
Education Programs in Theatre
Interactive & Reminiscence Theatre**

As growth continues in senior theatre, new learning opportunities are being offered by colleges, universities, and community organizations. Theatre practitioners are discovering how age integrated casts can bring new truth to the stage. Meanwhile, those in gerontology are seeing theatre as an excellent supplement to their activity program, as well as a dynamic therapeutic tool. In addition, young professionals are beginning to investigate senior theatre as a career. To meet these many needs, colleges and universities are creating academic programs to study the field in depth.

Seniors who have tasted the sweet flavor of success on stage are also wanting more eduction. Some simply wish to learn more about the many aspects of theatre while others are interested in studying plays and their structure, characters, and interpretation. Whatever their interest, they are finding community organizations willing to offer them insight. Many, such as *Elderhostel* or *Senior Ventures*, offer classes where students travel considerable distances to spend time studying theatre with their peers.

Acting on stage is only the beginning for some seniors. There has been a steady increase in the number of older models and performers who are being featured in films, commercials, and in some modeling. Both acting training and talent agencies which deal solely with mature performers are being created to fulfill the demand from the media.

Programs which combine social issues with theatre, such as reminiscence and interactive theatre continue to thrive as they attract audiences and participants wanting to use the arts to help others better understand the world around them. Even the use of drama therapy has been gaining new acceptance as practitioners come to understand how easily the arts can touch deeply hidden thoughts and feelings.

...And this is just the beginning of how many 'other' opportunities might be just around the corner! ✫

ACADEMIC PROGRAMS

Ohio State University

Ohio State University offers a Master Degree in Theatre with an interdisciplinary Certificate in Aging.

Dr. Joy Reilly
Department of Theatre
1089 Drake Union
Columbus, OH 43210
Phone: (614) 292-5821
Email: reilly.3@osu.edu

• • •

Montana State University - Billings

Montana State University offers a Minor in Theatre Therapy. The emphasis is on the use of theatre and gerontology in non-traditional settings. Students learn how to conduct programs in settings such as retirement homes, prisons, nursing homes, and in womens' and homeless shelters. Other students apply their skills on ranches for boys and girls who are physically challenged and emotionally disturbed. The course of study includes an internship, usually in nursing homes or other senior settings. A six-course curriculum completes the offerings which have helped graduates find employment in settings across the nation.

Montana State University - Billings
Dr. Victoria Coffman
Department of Communication & Theatre
1500 N. 30th
Billings, MT 59101-0298
Phone: (406) 657-2178

• • •

University of Nevada Las Vegas

UNLV offers a Bachelor of Arts in Senior Adult Theatre. It encompasses specialized courses in senior theatre. In addition, students earn a Certificate in Gerontology and have the opportunity to do extensive field work in senior theatre. As with most Bachelor of Arts programs, there are university core requirements such as math, science, and English. This degree prepares students of a variety of ages for up and coming careers that serve our burgeoning population of older adults.

University of Nevada Las Vegas
Dr. Ann McDonough
4505 S. Maryland Parkway
Las Vegas, NV 89154-5036
Phone: (702) 895-4248 / Fax: (702) 895-0833
Email: mdonoua@nevada.edu

ACTING IN COMMERCIALS

Senior Commercial Acting Program
Adrienne Omansky
4650 W. Olympic Blvd.
Los Angeles, CA 90019
Phone: (213) 737-2000 / Fax: (310) 556-3640

• • •

Mature Talent Enterprises
Mozelle Sims
620 Fifth Avenue West, #109
Seattle, WA 98119
Phone / Fax: (206) 283-3367
Email: bk806@scn.org

• • • •

"Acting in commercials makes me feel like I'm younger than I really am. When I'm on location, I meet people of all kinds and all ages and I'm always inspired – it lifts me up and give me a kick! I try to keep my image young, not with make-up, but from inside. Aging is not in my mind!"

Imogene Henderson, age 84, clown and performer in films and commercials. Photo by Patrick Burke in Best College Photography, 1996.

EDUCATION PROGRAMS IN THEATRE

Elderhostel
75 Federal Street
Boston, MA 02110-1941
Phone: (877) 426-8056 (toll free) / Fax: (877) 426-2166 (toll free)
Website: www.elderhostel.org

• • •

Institute for Readers Theatre
P.O. Box 17193
San Diego, CA 92177
Phone: (619) 276-1948 / Fax: (619) 576-7369
Email: info@readers-theatre.com
Website: www.readers-theatre.com

For summer session information contact:
University of Southern Maine
John LaBrie, Summer Session
37 College Avenue
Gorham, ME 04038
Phone: (207) 780-5422

INSTITUTE FOR READERS THEATRE

Dr. Bill Adams, Director

OFFERS

THE PERFECT SENIOR SOLUTION

SCRIPT SERVICE:
A catalog of pre-tested scripts ideal for use by Seniors. Our packets are full, easy-to-use instructional packets.

INTERNATIONAL WORKSHOPS:
For more than 25 years, the Institute has offered unique Readers Theatre experiences abroad. Join us for two memorable weeks of fun, recreation and learning in a family atmosphere while enjoying the exciting world of London Theatre.

Academic Sponsor:
UNIVERSITY OF SOUTHERN MAINE

IN SERVICES:
The Institute provides training for Seniors who want to organize an Readers Theatre group or improve the quality of performance in existing organizations. Half or full day and longer.

Institute for Readers Theatre
P.O. Box 17193
San Diego, CA 92177
Phone: (619) 276-1948
Fax: (619) 576-7369
Visit our Website!
www.readers-theatre.com
info@readers-theatre.com

Readers Theatre Script Service
P.O. Box 178333
San Diego, CA 92177
Phone / Fax: (619) 576-7369

John LaBrie, Summer Session
University of Southern Maine
37 College Avenue
Gorham, ME 04038
Phone: (207) 780-5422

EDUCATION PROGRAMS IN THEATRE *(Continued)*

The Institute for Therapy Through the Acts
Ted Rubenstein
7 Happ Road, Building A
Northfield, IL 60093
Phone: (847) 446-5364 / Fax: (847) 446-8458
Website: www.tmcns.com/ITA.html
Sponsor: The Music Center of North Shore

• • •

OASIS

OASIS is a national organization dedicated to enhancing the quality of life for older adults. Classes in acting, playwrighting, dance, music, and much more are offered five days a week at *OASIS* centers in May Company department stores such as Foley, Famous Barr, Filene's, Robinson-May, Hecht's, Lord and Taylor, L.S. Ayres, and Meier and Frank.

OASIS serves a national membership of more than 350,000 older adults in these 26 cities:

Akron, OH	Albuquerque, NM	Alton, IL
Chicago, IL	Cleveland, OH	Denver, CO
Enfield, CT	Escondido, CA	Eugene, OR
Gaithersburg, MD	Houston, TX	Hyattsville, MD
Indianapolis, IN	Los Angeles, CA	Oklahoma City, OK
Phoenix, AZ	Pittsburgh, PA	Portland, OR
Rochester, NY	St. Louis, MO	San Antonio, TX
San Diego, CA	Tucson, AZ	Washington D.C.

For more information on *OASIS* programs or how to become a member, check out *OASIS* online at http://www.oasisnet.org, or contact the *OASIS* center in the city nearest you.

The OASIS Institute
7710 Carondelet Avenue, Suite 125
St. Louis, MO 63105
Phone: (314) 862-2933 / Fax: (314) 862-2149
Website: www.oasisnet.org
Sponsor: May Department Store Company

• • • •

"My favorite is the drama classes. I always enjoyed drama and acting, but knew I could never make a living at it. Now that I'm a senior citizen, I can do drama!"

"I've taken clowning classes, acting classes, writing classes...it's great!"

"I feel more optimistic about life."

Comments from student evaluations after taking OASIS classes.

EDUCATION PROGRAMS IN THEATRE *(Continued)*

Senior Ventures
Southern Oregon University
Angela Decker
1250 Siskiyou Blvd.
Ashland, OR 97520
(800) 257-0577 or (541) 552-6285 / Fax: (541) 552-6380
Email: conferences@sou.edu
Website: http://www.sou.edu

REMINISCENCE THEATRE

Elders Share the Arts

Elders Share the Arts (ESTA) is a nationally recognized community arts organization founded in 1979, dedicated to validating personal histories, honoring diverse traditions, and connecting generations and cultures through the Arts. Through this unique synthesis of oral history and the creative arts, our staff of professional artists work with old and young to transform their life stories into dramatic, literary, and visual presentations which celebrate community life. Our touring storytellers and art exhibitions share the lifetime skills of older artists with communities that have little access to art. They work in neighborhood settings—senior centers, schools, nursing homes—throughout New York City. *ESTA's* Center for Creative Aging conducts training for professionals nationally and internationally.

Elders Share the Arts, Inc.
Susan Perlstein
72 East First Street
New York, NY 10003
Phone: (212) 780-1928 / Fax: (212) 529-5062
Email: elderarts@aol.com

INTERACTIVE THEATRE

The STOP-GAP Institute

The STOP-GAP method of Interactive Theatre was developed 20 years ago in weekly workshops with elders. Since 1978, STOP-GAP has added educational and therapeutic theatre programs for all ages to their weekly schedule. Currently, the company provides 1,300 interactive touring plays for students each year, as well as 600 drama therapy workshops, including many programs for elders. In addition, the STOP-GAP Institute trains allied professionals (such as teachers, counselors, and social workers) in their Interactive Theatre Method so that STOP-GAP based programs can be created outside of Southern California.

The STOP-GAP Institute
Don Lafoon & Victoria Bryan
1570 Brookhollow Drive, #114
Santa Ana, CA 92705
Phone: (714) 979-7061
Fax: (714) 979-7065
Email: Don Lafoon@stopgap.org
Website: www.stopgap.org

• • • •

"By teaching seniors to dance, I not only help them be more active, but I let our audiences see the depth of their knowledge and experience so younger people will realize seniors are the foundation of America and one of our most valuable resources. I'm building a better society!"

Bea Maggard used her training as a 6-year member of the Oregon Senior Theatre to capture the title of Ms. Senior Oregon.

ESTA

Elders Share The Arts, Inc.

Elders Share The Arts is a nationally recognized arts organization, dedicated to validating personal histories, honoring diverse traditions, and connecting generations and cultures through the Arts Through this unique synthesis of oral history and the creative arts, our staff of professional artists works with old and young to transform their life stories into dramatic, literary and visual presentations which celebrate community life. Our touring storytellers and art exhibitions share the lifetime skills of older artists with communities. We work in neighborhood settings - senior centers, schools, nursing homes -throughout New York City. ESTA trains professionals nationally and internationally through our Center for Creative Aging.

ESTA VIDEOS AND PUBLICATIONS

VIDEOS
ELDER VOICES, VHS, color, 26 minutes. Produced by Eric Breitbart. Brings viewers inside Living History Theater workshop sessions at Amsterdam Nursing Home in Manhattan. Provides moving portrait of a vital, caring and often humorous group of residents as they portray the stories of their lives. A training film for nursing home workers as well as an example of a Living History Theater program with frail elderly.

ARTS AND MINDS: BRIDGING BROOKLYN'S GENERATION GAP, VHS, 16 minutes. Produced by Wendy Cole. A short documentary on an ESTA intergenerational workshop involving school children and older adults from a neighboring senior center in Brooklyn.

ESTA PROFILE, VHS, color, 16 minutes. Produced by Hank Linhart. A short documentary on all Elders Share the Arts Programs including our living history workshops, Pearls of Wisdom storytellers and the Living History Theater Festivals.

AUDIO CASSETTE TAPES
PEARLS OF WISDOM Elder storytellers weave tales of struggle and triumph. (Live at Omega Institute conference on Aging) 30 minutes.

PUBLICATIONS
ESTA TRAINING MANUAL A 72-page comprehensive guide to running a Living History Theater workshop. Provides exercises in both reminiscence and theater.

GENERATING COMMUNITY: AN INTERGENERATIONAL PROGRAM THROUGH THE EXPRESSIVE ARTS
by Susan Perlstein with Jeff Bliss. Based on our award winning program, this book describes the step by step process of creating intergenerational partnerships between youth, seniors and arts agencies.

ORDER FORM

		No. of Copies	Amount
ELDER VOICES (Sale)	$50	_____	$_____
ARTS AND MINDS (Sale)	$30	_____	$_____
ESTA PROFILE (Sale)	$30	_____	$_____
PEARLS OF WISDOM	$8	_____	$_____
ESTA TRAINING MANUAL	$15	_____	$_____
A STAGE FOR MEMORY	$10	_____	$_____
GENERATING COMMUNITY	$20	_____	$_____
Subtotal		_____	$_____
Include $5 shipping/handling		$5.00	$_____
TOTAL		_____	$_____

Name_____Phone_____

Address_____

Make check payable to Elders Share the Arts:
72 East First Street, N.Y. 10003

72 East 1st Street   New York, NY 10003   (212) 780-1928

COMMUNITY THEATRES WITH SENIOR PROGRAMS

ommunity theatres are natural outlets for seniors who want to be either audience members or active participants. Their productions, which are usually selected because they meet the needs of a broad cross section of the community, often also appeal to seniors. In fact, many organizations consider the desires of their older audience members when selecting a production season. They know that seniors can be very dedicated and long-term patrons who attend each play like it was a habit!

But, community theatres do so much more. They welcome older thespians to take part on stage, appearing in roles which fit their age. It is a welcome joy for mature actors to share the footlights with people of all ages.

In addition, community theatres encourage older adults to participate back stage doing numerous tasks using their interests and talents to further the mission of the community theatre–which usually is to get the next play up and running! By being available during the day, when so many younger adults are working, seniors often perform routine tasks that keep the theatre functioning such as box office and publicity, filling the roles with dependability and skill.

The following community theatres provide programs for seniors which range from merely offering a senior discount to ones which have a fully staffed senior theatre program.

Additional community theatres can be found in the chapter on "Performing Groups," beginning on Page 7. ☆

Amlia Community Theatre
Linda McClane
P.O. Box 662
Fernandina Beach, FL 32035-0662

Anchorage Community Theatre, Inc.
Carole K. Green
P.O. Box 92147
Anchorage, AK 99509-2147

Arlington Friends of the Drama, Inc.
Cecia Couture
22 Academy Street
Arlington, MA 02476-6463

Asheville Community Theatre
Deborah R. Austin
35 E. Walnut Street
Asheville, NC 28801-2909

Bastrop Opera House
Chester Eitze
P.O. Box 691
Bastrop, TX 78602-0691

Bay City Players, Inc.
Jim Pawloski
P.O. Box 1
Bay City, MI 48707-0001

Belfry Players
Elizabeth W. Raker
P.O. Box 2714
Hendersonville, NC 28793-2714

Boise Actors' Guild
John T. Jones
9875 W. Florence Street
Boise, ID 83704-9229

Brevard Little Theatre
Joseph J. Carvajal
P.O. Box 544
Brevard, NC 28712-0544

C.A.S.T.
Judie Handel
P.O. Box 215
Hood River, OR 97031

Cedar Falls Community Theatre
John C. Luzaich
103 Main Street
P.O. Box 381
Cedar Falls, IA 50613-0381

Charleston Working Theatre, Inc.
Kristin Johnson
442 Bunker Hill Street
Charlestown, MA 02129-1718

Chatham Community Players
Richard Hennessy
23 N. Passaic Avenue
P.O. Box 234
Chatham, NJ 07928-0234

Cheyenne Little Theatre Players
Randy Oestman
P.O. Box 20087
Cheyenne, WY 82003-7002

Cockpit in Court Summer Theatre
F. Scott Black
7201 Rossville Blvd.
Baltimore, MN 21237-3855

Community Actors of Saint Bernard
Jude Poloma
P.O. Box 1024
Chalmette, LA 70044-1024

Community Light Opera and Theatre
Deanna Ripley-Lotee
P.O. Box 957
Ridgecrest, CA 93556-0957

Community Theatre League
Andree Phillips
454 Pine Street
Williamsport, PA 17701-6200

Community Theatre Guild, Inc.
Eric Brant
P.O. Box 167
Valparaiso, IN 46384-0167

Creative Productions, Inc.
Walter L. Born
2 Beaver Place
Matawan, NJ 07747-2303

Danville Light Opera
Nancy Henderson
P.O. Box 264
Danville, Il 61834-0264

Denver Civic Theatre
Henry Lowenstein
721 Santa Fe Drive
Denver, CO 80204-4428

Department of the Army Music & Theatre
USACFSC, Attn: Army Entertainment 4th
Jerold J. Paquette
Summit Centre, 4700 King Street
Alexandria, VA 22302-4418

Detroit Theatre Organ Society
Don Jenks
6424 Michigan Avenue
Detroit, MI 48210-2957

Downtown Drama Company
Bill Hertz
105 S. 3rd
P.O. Box 15
Laurens, IA 50554-0015

Dudley Riggs Creative Services
Dudley Riggs
1586 Burton Street
Saint Paul, MN 55108-1301

East Essex Players
Mrs. J.M. Byrne
169 Tankerville Drive
Leigh-on Sea
Essex SS9 3DB England

Enter Laughing, Inc.
Diana Forsha
2873 Chancery Lane
Clearwater, FL 33759-1427

Epilogue Players
Sandra Williams
8014 Clearwater Pkwy.
Indianapolis, IN 46240

Fargo-Morehead Community Theatre
Bruce Tinker
333 4th Street, S.
Fargo, ND 58103-1913

FATE Productions
Cheryl Richter
82 Barholm Avenue
Stamford, CT 06907-1304

Fernandina Little Theatre
Kate Hart
P.O. Box 553
Fernandina Beach, FL 32035-0553

First Avenue Playhouse-Starburst
Joe Bagnole
123 First Avenue
Atlantic Highlands, NJ 07716-1240

Flint Community Players, Inc.
Steven Mokofsky
2462 South Ballanger Hwy.
Flint, MI 48507

Fort Smith Little Theatre
Sonda Foti
P.O. Box 3752
Fort Smith, AR 72913-3752

Fort Wayne Civic Theatre, Inc.
Al Franklin
303 E. Main Street
Fort Wayne, IN 46802-1907

Fourth of July Creek Productions
Walton Jones
1010 1/2 Brent Avenue
South Pasadena, CA 91030-3390

Frisco Community Theatre
Aileen Roberts
P.O. Box 1221
Frisco, TX 75034-1221

Gaslight Theatre
Lendl Detwiler
221 N. Independence Street
Enid, OK 73701-4010

Grand Opera House
Susan J. Reidel
135 W. 8th Street
P.O. Box 632
Dubuque, IA 52004-0632

Greater Grand Forks Community Theatre
Steve Saari
Fire Hall Theatre
412 2nd Avenue, N.
Grand Forks, ND 58203-3710

Green Earth Players
Fred Manfred
P.O. Box 856
Luverne, MN 56156

Greenwood Community Theatre
Myra Greene Shaffer
110 Kingston
Greenwood, SC 29649-9569

● ●

Harbor Playhouse
Bennie Nipper
3803 Highway 3
Dickinson, TX 77539-5158

Huntington Playhouse
Tom Meyrose
P.O. Box 770056
Lakewood, OH 44107-0012

Ice House Theatre
Paul Bengston
P.O. Box 759
Mount Dora, FL 32756-0759

Ichabod's Little Theatre in the Hollow
Mary Olendorf
P.O. Box 652
South Haven, MI 49090-0652

Illinois Theatre Association
Wallace Smith
1225 W. Belmont Avenue
Chicago, IL 60657-3205

Johnson City Community Theatre
Charles B. Jones
P.O. Box 452
Johnson City, TN 37605-0452

Joplin Little Theatre
Cindy Cloud
P.O. Box 374
Joplin, MO 64802-0374

Kenneth Scott Vocal Theatre, Inc.
Susan Down
1809 Sierra Valley Way
Las Vegas, NV 89128-3038

Lakeland Cultural Arts Center
Walter K. Hurst
P.O. Box 130
Littleton, NC 27850-0130

Largo Cultural Center
Donna McBride
P.O. Box 296
Largo, FL 33779-0296

Le Mars Community Theatre
Marlene Fitzpatrick
P.O. Box 45
Le Mars, IA 51031-0045

Little Theatre of Monroe, Inc.
Pat S. Hoover
P.O. Box 4822
Monroe, LA 71211-4822

Little Town Players
Nancy Johnson
P.O. Box 437
Bedford, VA 24523-0437

Manatee Players
Robert Prescott
102 12th Street, W.
Bradenton, FL 34205-7815

Marin Shakespeare Company
Lesley S. Currier
P.O. Box 4053
San Rafael, CA 94913
Phone: (415) 499-1108
Fax: (415) 499-1492
Email: lesley@linex.com
Website: www.marinShakespeare.org

Market House Theatre
Michael Cochran
141 Kentucky Avenue
Paducah, KY 42003-1554

Melbourne Civic Theatre
Nancy Hudack
P.O. Box 1543
Melbourne, FL 32902-1534

Meridian Little Theatre
Jummy Pigford
P.O. Box 3157
Meridian, MS 39303-3157

Mira Theatre Guild
Angie Gant Oninski
P.O. Box 7585
Vallejo, CA 94590-1585

Mount Prospect Theatre Society
Randy Toelke
420 Dempster Avenue
Mount Prospect, IL 60056-5702

Naples Players, Inc.
Joyce Heptner
P.O. Box 668
Naples, FL 34106-0668

Nomads Theatre Workshop
Melissa E. Taylor
P.O. Box 76571
Washington, D.C. 20013-6571

Ocala Civic Theatre
Mary Britt
P.O. Box 2132
Ocala, FL 34470

Octad-One Productions, Inc.
Wayne Alan Erreca
10009 Maine Avenue
Lakeside, CA 92040

Oklahoma Community Theatre Association
Kay Armstrong
120 N. Robinson Avenue, #1805
Oklahoma City, OK 73102-7400

Pensacola Little Theatre, Inc.
Donna Peoples
400 S. Jefferson Street
Pensacola, FL 32501-5902

Peoria Players Theatre
Nicki E. Haschke
4300 N. University Street
Peoria, IL 61614-5823

Performing Arts Society of Nevada
John Meren
6301 Malachite Bay Avenue
Las Vegas, NV 89130-3712

Players Guild of Canton, The
Kris Furlan, Managing Director
1001 Market Avenue, N.
Canton, OH 44702-1024
Phone: (330) 453-7617
Fax: (330) 452-4477
Website: www.playersguildofcanton.com

Quannapowitt Players
Donna Corbett
55 Hopkins Street
Reading, MA 01867-3917

Quincy Community Theatre
Barbara Rowell
300 Civic Center Plaza, Ste. 118
Quincy, IL 62301-4139

Reston Community Players
Sue Pinkman
2310 Colts Neck Road
Reston, VA 20191-2886

River's Bend Playhouse, Inc.
Geoff D. Leonard
P.O. Box 5112
Evansville, IN 47716-5112

Rockwall Community Playhouse
Darlene Singleton
P.O. Box 2031
Rockwall, TX 75087-4431

San Luis Obispo Little Theatre
Cynthia Anthony
P.O. Box 122
San Luis Obispo, CA 93406-0122

San Pedro Playhouse
Francis W. Elborne
P.O. box 12356
San Antonio, TX 78212-0356

Southwest Playhouse Fine Arts Center
Mike Perkins
P.O. Box 204
Clinton, OK 73601-0204

Stage Coach Players
Bernie Schuneman
P.O. Box 511
De Kalb, IL 60115-0511

Stage Crafters Community Theatre
Craig Ewing
P.O. box 1749
Fort Walton Beach, FL 32549-1749

**Staten Island Shakespearean
    Theatre Co.**
Craig Stoebling
126 Cassidy Place #N
Staten Island, NY 10301-1182

Sterling Playmakers
Terry DiMurro
22373 Stablehouse Drive
Sterling, VA 20164-5327

Temple Civic Theatre
Delores Rosen
2413 S. 13th Street
Temple, TX 76504-7547

Theatre Company of Rhode Island
Michael Thurber
508 Tourtellot Hill Road
Chepachet, RI 02814-2125

Theatre in the Park
Allen Reep
107 Pullen Road
Raleigh, NC 27607-7367

Theatre of Western Springs
4384 Hampton Avenue
Western Springs, IL 60558-1338

Theatre Cedar Rapids
Richard Barker
102 3rd Street, SE
Cedar Rapids, IA 52401-1246

Theatre Winterhaven
Norman M. Small
P.O. Box 1230
Winter Haven, FL 33882-1230

Theatre Works
Julia Thomson
9850 W. Peoria Avenue
Peoria, AZ 85345-6110

Theatrikos
Jonathan Beller
11 W. Cherry Avenue
Flagstaff, AZ 86001-4517

Topeka Civic Theatre
Shannon Reilly
534 1/2 N. Kansas Avenue
Topeka, KS 66608-1238

**Township Center for the
    Performing Arts**
Edward Meszaros
2452 Lyons Road
Coconut Creek, FL 33063

Trumbull New Theatre
Debra Godiciu
5883 Youngstown Road
P.O. Box 374
Warren, OH 44482-0374

Twin Cities Players, Inc.
Larry Nielsen
P.O. Box 243
St. Joseph, MI 49085-0243

Venice Little Theatre
Murray Chase
140 Tampa Avenue, W.
Venice, FL 34285-1796

Waimea Community Theatre
Michael Bray
P.O. box 1660
Kamuela, HI 96743-1660
Phone: (808) 885-5018 (message) or
    (808) 885-7875
Email: wct@theoffice.net
Website: www.theoffice.net/wct

**Valley of the Stars Community
    Theatre**
Randall Read
Drawer 1609
Studio City, CA 91611-1609
Phone: (818) 513-7501

Victory Players
56 Harvard Street
Holyoke, MA 01040-2023

Village Players, Inc.
Beverly Bell
P.O. Box 5184
Bella Vista, AR 72714-0184

ASSOCIATIONS IN ARTS & AGING

hough there are many associations which are allied with either theatre, the arts, or aging, there are only a select few that combine these areas. Below is a listing of some of them:

American Association of Community Theatre
Julie Angelo
4712 Enchanted Oaks
College Station, TX 77845-7649
Phone: (409) 744-0611
Fax: (409) 776-8718
Email: info@aact.org
Website: www.aact.org

American Society on Aging (ASA)
833 Market Street, Ste. 511
San Francisco, CA 94103-1824
Phone: (415) 974-9600
Fax: (415) 974-0300
Email: info@asa.asaging.org
Website: www.asaging.org

Arts and Healing Network
3450 Sacramento Street
Box 612
San Francisco, CA 94118
Fax: (415) 771-3696
Website: www.artheals.org

American Association of Community Colleges
1 Dupont Circle NW, Ste. 410
Washington DC 20036
Phone: (202) 728-0200
Fax: (202) 833-2467
Website: www.aacc.nche.edu

Americans for the Arts
1000 Vermont Avenue, 12th Floor
Washington D.C. 20005-2304
Phone: (202) 371-2830
Fax: (202) 371-0424
Email: ifa@citenet.net
Website: www.ifa-fiv.org

Association for Gerontology in Higher Education
1030 15th Street, NW, Ste. 240
Washington D.C. 20005-1503
Phone: (202) 289-9806/ /Fax: (202) 289-9824
Email: aghetemp@aghe.org
Website: www.aghe.org
(Association is a unit of the Gerontological Society of America–GSA.)

Association for Theatre and Disability
Olivia Raynor, Ph.D., OTR
National Arts and Disability Center
300 UCLA Medical Plaza, Ste. 330
Box 956967
Los Angeles, CA 90095-6967
Phone: (310) 794-1141 / Fax: (310) 794-1143
Email: oraynor@mednet.ucla.edu
Website: www.npi.ucla.edu/ata/

Educational Theatre Association
Don LaFleche
2343 Auburn Avenue
Cincinnati, OH 45219-2819
Phone: (513) 421-3900 / Fax: (513) 421-7077
Email: dlafleche@etassoc.org
Website: www.etassoc.org

International Arts Medicine Association
714 Old Lancaster Road
Bryn Mawr, PA 19010
Phone: (610) 525-3784
Fax: (610) 525-3250
Email: IAMA@aol.com
Website: http://members.aol.com/iamaorg/

International Federation on Ageing
425 Viger Avenue, West, Ste. 520
Montreal, Quebec, Canada H2Z 1X2
Phone: (514) 396-3358
Fax: (514) 396-3378
Email: ifa@citenet.net
Website: www.ifa-fiv.org

National Association for Drama Therapy (NADT)

5505 Connecticut Avenue, NW #280
Washington D.C. 20015
Phone: (202) 966-7409
Fax: (202) 966-2283
Email: nadt@danielgrp.com
Website: www.nadt.org

National Association for Poetry Therapy (APT)

5505 Connecticut Avenue, NW #280
Washington D.C. 20015
Phone: (202) 966-2536
Email: rdaniel@his.com
Website: www.poetrytherapy.org

National Coalition of Arts Therapies Association (NCATA)

2117 L. Street, NW #274
Washington D.C. 20037
Phone: (202) 678-6787
Website: www.ncata.com

National Council on the Aging

409 Third Street, SW Ste. 200
Washington D.C. 20024
Phone: (800) 424-9046 or
   (202) 479-1200
Fax: (202) 479-0735
Email: info@ncoa.org
Website: www.ncoa.org

National Movement Theatre Association

Kari Margolis
115 Washington Avenue, N.
Minneapolis, MN 55401
Phone: (612) 339-4709

New England Theatre Conference

c/o Department of Theatre
Northeastern University
360 Huntington Avenue
Boston, MA 02115
Fax: (617) 424-1057
Email: netc@world.std.com

Senior Theatre Research & Performance

Association of Theatre in Higher Education
906 Lacey Avenue #218
Lisle, IL 60532-2303
Phone: (630) 964-5555
Website: www.accad.ohio-state.edu/~jreilly

Society for the Arts in Healthcare

3867 Tennyson Street
Denver, CO 80212-2107
Phone: (800) 243-1233 or
   (303) 433-4446
Fax: (303) 433-0002
Email: healtharts@uoli.com
Website: www.societyartshealthcare.org

Very Special Arts

1300 Connecticut Avenue, NW #700
Washington D.C. 20036
Phone: (202) 628-2800
Fax: (202) 737-0725
Website: www.vsarts.org

85

hen adapted to film and video, senior performing blends visual effect with the words of the senior participants and the emotional impact of a performance to make a dynamic statement. It is an art form which is well suited for the media.

Films and videos featuring senior performing have received much critical acclaim. *Close Harmony*, a story about an intergenerational chorus, won an Academy Award. Next, *I Was Young, Now I'm Wonderful* was awarded an Emmy. Then, in 1998, *Still Kicking: The Fabulous Palm Springs Follies*, was nominated for an Academy Award in the Short Documentary category. It was followed by another senior theatre film, *The Personals: Improvisations on Romance in the Golden Years*, which in 1999, was the Academy Award winner for best documentary short subject.

Whether film and video is used to document a project or to make a training CD-ROM for physicians, the medium is quite powerful. Below are several sources of senior theatre film and videos. ✰

Elders Share the Arts (ESTA)

Arts and Minds: Bridging Brooklyn's Generation Gap
A short documentary on an ESTA intergenerational workshop involving school children and older adults from a senior center in Brooklyn, New York. Video, 16 mins. Sale $30.

ESTA Profile
A short documentary on the *Elders Share the Arts* programs including their living history workshops, *Pearls of Wisdom* storytellers and the *Living History Theatre Festivals*. VHS, color, 16 mins. Sale $30.

Elder Voices
This video brings viewers inside *Living History Theatre* workshop sessions at Amsterdam Nursing Home in Manhattan. It provides a moving portrait of a vital, caring, and often humorous group of residents as they portray the stories of their lives. Video, 26 min. Sale $50.

Elders Share the Arts (ESTA)
72 East First Street
New York, NY 10003-9322
Phone: (212) 780-1928
Fax: (212) 529-5062
Email: elderarts@aol.com

Fanlight Productions

The Arts in Healthcare
This video looks at the role of the arts in healthcare and profiles several programs that integrate art into healing. Winner of Third Place, Association for Death Education and Counseling. 28 mins.

The Personals: Improvisations on Romance in the Golden Years
1999 Academy Award-winner for Best Documentary Short Subject! A drama group for senior citizens performs an original play at a community theater on Manhattan's Lower East Side. Drawn from comedy and drama of their lives, the play features elderly people looking for dates through the personal ads. Directed by Keiko Ibi, this was her first Academy Award nomination and her first win! Rental $50.

Fanlight Productions
47 Halifax Street
Boston, MA 02130
Phone: (800) 937-4113
Fax: (617) 524-8838
Outside the U.S., call (617) 524-0980
Email: fanlight@fanlight.com
Website: www.fanlight.com

Filmakers Library

Art With Elders in Long Term Care
A serious art program for elders, aimed at developing talented people over eighty, the film was created at the Hillhaven Convalescent Hospital. Using life histories, they create works of art. Techniques are adaptable to working with older adults in other contexts. Produced by Mary Ann Merker-Benton. Video only, 10 mins. Sale $150. Rental $35.

Close Harmony
This Academy Award-winning film is a delightfully warm documentary about a senior citizens' chorus and an elementary school chorus who join for a combined concert. From rehearsals to the concert, a bond forms creating a magical performance. Video, 30 mins. Sale $195.00 Rental $55.

The Women of Hodson: Sharing Life Experiences Through Drama
The Hodson Senior Citizen Center is the setting for a unique program of improvisational theater where they develop and perform original works based on their own life experiences. Their stories reflect their rich individual histories. Social workers, recreation therapists, gerontologists, and theatre teachers will find this a stimulating film. Video, 30-minutes, 16 mm. Sale $450; Rental $55.

Filmakers Library
124 East 40th Street
New York, NY 10016
Phone: (212) 808-4980
Fax: (212) 808-4983
Email: info@filmakers.com
Website: www.filmakers.com

Janice Kaminsky

Still Kicking: The Fabulous Palm Spring Follies

An inspirational chronicle of a chorus line of feisty senior citizens who will dazzle you with their talent and energy level. Playing 10 shows a week to sold-out crowds, this 39-minute documentary follows the performers, ages 58 to 80, from auditions to opening day, interspersed with interviews. It was directed by Mel Damski, who also directs "Ally McBeal," and was nominated for the 1998 Academy Award in the category of Documentary Short Subject.

Janice Kaminsky
358 Via Altamira
Palm Springs, CA 92262
Phone: (760) 320-5722
Fax: (760) 322-7716
Email: jkaccess@aol.com

Joy Reilly

The Golden Stage

This 30-minute film highlights the therapeutic effects of seniors performing on stage and features members of *Grandparents Living Theatre*. Produced in 1988.

I Was Young, Now I'm Wonderful

This Emmy Award-winning film was produced by *Grandparents Living Theatre*, introduced by Bernadine Heeley. It's a thirty-minute performance in a one-hour film. Produced in 1996.

In The Heartland

A six-minute documentary, featured on World News Tonight from ABC Television, highlights *Grandparents Living Theatre*. Produced in 1995.

Joy Reilly
Ohio State University
Columbus, OH 43220
Phone: (614) 457-5765
Email: reilly.3@osu.edu

Stagebridge

Friends and Lovers
Four scenes about older people in love are performed by the *College Avenue Players*, aged 65 to 84. It includes live performance with original music and introductions to each scene. Video, 30 mins.

Stagebridge on TV
This videotape highlights performances of "*Grandparents Tales,*" the Storytelling in the Schools Program, and acting and storytelling classes for seniors. The performances appeared previously on CNN, World Monitor TV, and KGO-TV. Video, 30 mins. Sale $25.

Stagebridge
2501 Harrison Street
Oakland, CA 94612
Phone: (510) 444-4755

Kate Wilkinson

The Clinical Diagnosis of Alzheimer's Disease: An Interactive Guide for Family Physicians
Target Theatre Society appeared in this CD-ROM to help physicians improve both their diagnostic techniques and their relationships with older patients. Produced by Dr. Harry Karlinsky for the Riverview Hospital in Vancouver BC, Canada.

Kate Wilkinson
558 Selkirk Avenue
Victoria BC V9A 2T1
Canada
Phone: (250) 383-0003

• • • •

"The best thing about working with senior actors is that they have a great deal of life experience to draw from, both for ideas and for empathy. Also, generally speaking, they sense that there is too little time left to waste it on ego nonsense; they'd rather enjoy the working process than argue over details."

Kate Wilkinson, Past Director, Victoria Target Theatre Society, Victoria BC, Canada.

Terra Nova Films

Terra Nova Films produces and distributes films and videos exclusively about elderhood issues. Films like *My Mother, My Father, Curtain Call, Flowers for Charlie, Grandparents Raising Grandchildren, Complaints of a Dutiful Daughter*, and *Harvest of Age*, all challenge stereotypical perceptions and attitudes about older adulthood and celebrate creativity, resilience, knowledge, and experience of older adults.

Terra Nova Films also coordinates an annual Film Festival. The only festival of its kind in the United States, the **Silver Images Film Festival**, showcases films and videos that celebrate older adulthood. The festival is recognized both by local film critics and by audiences as being "*a refreshing alternative*" and of "*high quality*" (Michael Wilmington, Chicago Tribune). Film and video entries are accepted on an ongoing basis.

A One & A Two
This is a portrait of Angelo, a widower, who after thirty-seven years of marriage begins to build a new life as a ballroom dancer. 27 min. Video. Sale $195. Rental $55.

Acting Up
A documentary which studies the development of an impromptu drama group composed of non-professional actors over the age of 65, offers educational and instructional material for others seeking to duplicate this improvisational approach to senior theatre. 30 minutes.

Whisper, the Waves, the Wind
This unique and lyrical film uses performance art to cast off stereotypes of aging and gender barriers and see older women in a new light. "*Suzanne Lacy's ceremonial tribute to feminine wisdom is an extraordinary film, an absolutely delightful experience*," says Landers Film Review. Video, 28 mins. Sale $295. Rental $55.

Terra Nova Films
James Vanden Bosch
9848 S. Winchester Avenue
Chicago, IL 60643
Phone: (800) 779-8491 or
   (773) 881-8491
Fax: (773) 881-3368
Email: tnf@terranova.org
Website: www.terranona.org

Scene from *"Flowers for Charlie."*

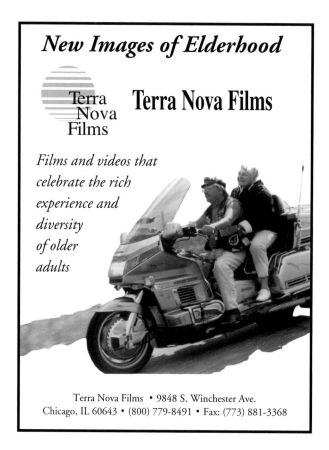
• • • •

**"I like being on stage –
I'm a show off !"**

*Edith Phipps, an 11 year
participant in Oregon &
Northwest Senior Theatre.*

FUNDING FOR SENIOR THEATRE

*T*his chapter on funding is the last one in the book because it is the element in Senior Theatre which could be improved for so many performing groups. Though many are able to fulfill their missions, most suffer due to inadequate budgets. Thus, their creativity, productivity, professionalism and many other factors are limited simply due to the lack of money. Our hope is that *Senior Theatre Connections* will encourage performing groups to seek more extensive funding so they can expand their programming and administrative support in an effort to increase the visibility of this new theatre genre.

Actually, senior performing groups are fortunate because so many are already affiliated with nonprofit organizations. Thus, increased funding might be as close as the local community theatre, community college, professional theatre, aging organization, or arts group which is already providing a close and supportive relationship.

The one constant in the area of funding is that it requires a continual and exhaustive search for new sources while fostering ever stronger relationships with current funders.

The sources listed are places to begin. Also included is information about state and regional arts organizations which can be beneficial partners, able to supply a wealth of information. Remember that local donations, endowments, and other gifts are excellent for long-term and often easily obtained funding. Finally, the Internet is a superb resource with ever-expanding listings to aid nonprofit organizations.

Good luck, grow strong, and continue to spread the message to both audiences and funding sources that seniors appearing on stage is beneficial to the culture and for both audiences and performers alike – it's better than a trip to the doctor! ☆

The Grantsmanship Center
1125 W. 6th Street, 5th Floor
P.O. Box 17220
Los Angeles, CA 90017
Phone: (213) 482-9860
Fax: (213) 482-9863
Email: norton@tgci.com
Website: www.tgci.com

Independent Sector
1828 L. Street, N.W.
Washington D.C. 20036
Phone: (202) 223-8100
Fax: (202) 416-0580
Website: www.indepsec.org

The Foundation Center
79 5th Avenue, 16th Floor
New York, NY 10003-3076
Phone: (212) 620-4230 or
　(800) 424-9836
Fax: (212) 807-3677
Online librarian: library@fdncenter.org
Website: www.fdncenter.org

PEN American Center
568 Broadway
New York, NY 10012-3225
Fax: (212) 334-2181
Email: JM@PEN.ORG

The *Pen American Center* publishes an excellent resource for writers, "*Grants and Awards Available to American Writers*," which contains 1,000 listings and 248 awards. The drama category is quite extensive and includes many production opportunities for playwrights.

INTERNET RESOURCES

Below is a general overview of some additional websites which provide information about grants. They often provide links to major funding opportunities, data bases, and professional activities which may be of use in a search for funding.

Arts Funding
Website: www.artslynx.org/funding.htm

The Chronical of Philanthropy
Website: http://philanthropy.com

Foundations On-Line
Website: www.foundations.org

The Grants Information Center
website: http://sra.rams.com

Grant Getter's Guide to the Internet
Website: www.mindspring.com/-ajgrant/guide.htm

Grant Writing and Fund Raising Information Resources
Website: http://omega.geron.uga.edu/grants.html

Internet Nonprofit Center
Website: www.nonprofits.org

National Endowment for the Arts
Website: http://arts.endow.gov

Philanthropy Journal Online
Website: www.philanthropyjournal.org

Polaris
Website: http://polarisgrantscentral.net/

STATE ARTS AGENCIES

It is important to capitalize on the immense amount of information available from local, state, and regional arts agencies. They serve as clearinghouses and are usually up-to-date about funding opportunities. Arts agency personnel should become acquainted with senior performing programs, appreciative of the art form, and, equally important, the contributions which elders make to the arts.

Another reason to contact your state arts agency is that each one has a *504 Coordinator* who can help you understand and interpret assessibility regulations. They make sure your work accommodates people with disabilities.

Alabama State Council on the Arts
201 Monroe Street
Montgomery, AL 36130-1800
Phone: (334) 242-4076
Fax: (334) 240-3269

Alaska State Council on the Arts
411 West 4th Avenue, Suite 1E
Anchorage, AK 99501-2343
Phone: (970) 269-6610
Fax: (970) 269-6601
Email: helen@aksca.org

American Samoa Council on Culture, Arts and Humanities
P.O. Box 1540
Office of the Governor
Pago Pago, AS 96799
Phone: (684) 633-4347
Fax: (684) 633-2059

Arizona Commission on the Arts
417 West Roosevelt Street
Phoenix, AZ 85003
Phone: (602) 255-5882
Fax: (602) 256-0282
Email: artscomm@primenet.com

Arkansas Arts Council
1500 Tower Building
323 Center Street
Little Rock, AR 72201
Phone: (501) 324-9770
Fax: (501) 324-9154
Email: info@dah.state.ar.us

California Arts Council

1300 I Street, Ste. 930
Sacramento, CA 95814
Phone: (916) 322-6555
Fax: (916) 322-6575
Email: cac@cwo.com

Colorado Council of the Arts

750 Pennsylvania Street
Denver, CO 80203-3699
Phone: (303) 894-2617
Fax: (303) 894-2615
Email: coloarts@is.netcom.com

Connecticut Commission on the Arts

Gold Building
755 Main Street
Hartford, CT 06103
Phone: (860) 566-4770
Fax: (860) 566-6462
Email: LKARDOK@csl.ctstateu.edu

Delaware Division of the Arts

Carvel State Office Building
820 North French Street, 5th Floor
Wilmington, DE 19801
Phone: (302) 577-8278
Fax: (302) 577-6561
Email: delarts@artswire.org

• • • •

"It is seldom that one can choose a new career after retirement, particularly one as rewarding as senior theatre. As well as giving me a new lease on life in a totally different direction, I have found the companionship and caring of such a group to be a major feature in the enjoyment of my retirement."

Tom Hardwick, Member of the Oregon Senior Theatre and the Northwest Senior Theatre.

*District of Columbia Commission on
    the Arts and Humanities*
415 12th Street N.W., Suite 804
Washington D.C. 20004
Phone: (202) 724-5613
Fax: (202) 727-4135
Email: dccah@erols.com

Florida Division of Cultural Affairs
Department of State, The Capitol
Tallahassee, FL 32399-0250
Phone: (850) 487-2980
Fax: (850) 922-5259

Georgia Council for the Arts
260 14th Street N.W., Suite 401
Atlanta, GA 30318
Phone: (404) 685-2787
Fax: (404) 685-2788
Email: gca@gwins.campus.mci.net

Guam Council on the Arts and Humanities
P.O. Box 2950
Agana, GU 96910
Phone: (671) 475-2242
Fax: (671) 472-2871
Email: gcaha@kuentos.guam.net

Hawaii Foundation on Culture and the Arts
44 Merchant Street
Honolulu, HI 96813
Phone: (808) 586-0300
Fax: (808) 568-0308
email: sfca@sfca.hi.us

Idaho Commission on the Arts
P.O. Box 83720
Boise, ID 83720-0008
Phone: (208) 334-2119
Fax: (208) 334-2488
Email: fhebert@ica.state.id.us

Illinois Arts Council
100 West Randolph Street
Suite 10-500
Chicago, IL 60601
Phone: (312) 814-6750
Fax: (312) 814-1471
Email: ilarts@state.il.us

Indiana Arts Commission
402 W. Washington Street, Rm. W072
Indianapolis, IN 46204
Phone: (317) 232-1268
Fax: (317) 232-5595
Email: InArtsComm@aol.com

Iowa Arts Council
Capitol Complex
600 E. Locust
Des Moines, IA 50319
Phone: (515) 281-4451
Fax: (515) 242-6498
Email: wjackso@max.state.ia.us

Kansas Arts Commission
Jayhawk Tower
700 S.W. Jackson, Suite 1004
Topeka, KS 66603
Phone: (785) 296-3335
Fax: (785) 296-4989

Kentucky Arts Council
31 Fountain Place
Frankfort, KY 40601
Phone: (502) 564-3757
Fax: (502) 564-2839
Email: kyarts@arts.smag.state.ky.us

Louisiana Division of the Arts
P.O. Box 44247
Baton Rouge, LA 70804
Phone: (504) 342-8180
Fax: (504) 342-8173
Email: arts@crt.state.la.us

Maine Arts Commission
55 Capitol Street
State House Station 25
Augusta, ME 04333
Phone: (207) 287-2724
Fax: (207) 287-2335
Email: alden.wilson@state.me.us

Maryland State Arts Council
601 North Howard Street, 1st Floor
Baltimore, MD 21201
Phone: (410) 767-6555
Fax: (410) 333-1062
Email: jbackas@mdbusiness.state.md.us

Massachusetts Cultural Council
120 Boylston Street, 2nd Floor
Boston, MA 02116-4600
Phone: (617) 727-3668
Fax: (617) 727-0044
Email: Mary@art.state.ma.us

Michigan Council for Arts and Cultural Affairs
1200 Sixth Street, 11th Floor
Detroit, MI 48226-2461
Phone: (313) 256-3731
Fax: (313) 256-3781
Email: betty.boone@cis.state.mi.us

Minnesota State Arts Board
Park Square Court
400 Sibley Street, Suite 200
St. Paul, MN 55102
Phone: (612) 215-1600
Fax: (612) 215-1602
Email: msab@state.mn.us

Mississippi Arts Commission
239 North Lamar Street, 2nd Floor
Jackson, MS 39201
Phone: (601) 359-6030 or 6040
Fax: (601) 359-6008
Email: bradley@arts.state.ms.us

Missouri Arts Council
111 North 7th Street, Suite 105
St. Louis, MO 63101
Phone: (314) 340-6845
Fax: (314) 340-7215
Email: mac@artswire.org

Montana Arts Council
City County Building
316 North Park Avenue, Suite 252
Helena, MT 59620-2201
Phone: (406) 444-6430
Fax: (406) 444-6548
Email: mtarts@initco.net

Nebraska Arts Council
Joslyn Castle Carriage House
3838 Davenport
Omaha, NE 68131-2329
Phone: (402) 595-2122
Fax: (402) 595-2334
Email: nacart@synergy.net

Nevada Arts Council
602 North Curry Street
Carson City, NV 89703
Phone: (702) 687-6680
Fax: (702) 687-6688

New Hampshire State Council on the Arts
40 North Main Street
Concord, NH 03301-4974
Phone: (603) 271-2789
Fax: (603) 271-3584
Email: rlawrence@nhsa.state.nh.us

New Jersey State Council on the Arts
P.O. Box 306
Trenton, NJ 08625-0306
Phone: (609) 292-6130
Fax: (609) 989-1440
Email: barbara@arts.sos.state.nj.us

New Mexico Arts
228 East Palace Avenue
Santa Fe, NM 87501
Phone: (505) 827-6490
Fax: (505) 827-6043

New York State Council on the Arts
915 Broadway, 8th Floor
New York, NY 10010
Phone: (212) 387-7000
Fax: (212) 387-7164
Email: nclark@nysca.org

North Carolina Arts Council
Department of Cultural Resources
Raleigh, NC 27611
Phone: (919) 733-2821
Fax: (919) 733-4834
Email: mregan@ncacmail.dcr.state.nc.us

North Dakota Council on the Arts
418 East Broadway, Suite 70
Bismarck, ND 58501-4086
Phone: (701) 328-3954
Fax: (701) 328-3963
Email: ndca@artswire.org

Commonwealth Council for Arts and Culture (North Mariana Islands)
P.O. Box 5553, CHRB
Saipan, MP 96950
Phone: 011-670-322-9982 or 9983
Fax: 011-670-322-9028
Email: galaidi@gtepacifica.net

Ohio Arts Council
727 East Main Street
Columbus, OH 43205
Phone: (614) 466-2613
Fax: (614) 466-4494
Email: jamig@mail.oac.ohio.gov

Oklahoma Arts Council
P.O. Box 52001-2001
Oklahoma City, OK 73152-2001
Phone: (405) 521-2931
Fax: (405) 521-6418
Email: okarts@tmn.com

Oregon Arts Commission
775 Summer Street, N.E.
Salem, OR 97310
Phone: (503) 986-0087
Fax: (503) 986-0260
Email: Oregon.ArtsComm@State.OR.US
Website: www.das.state.or.us/OAC/

Pennsylvania Council on the Arts
Finance Building, Room 216
Harrisburg, PA 17120
Phone: (717) 787-6883
Fax: (717) 783-2538
Email: phorn@arts.cmicpo1.state.pa.us

Institute of Puerto Rican Culture
P.O. Box 9024184
San Juan, PR 00902-4184
Phone: (787) 725-5137
Fax: (787) 724-8393

Rhode Island State Council on the Arts
95 Cedar Street, Suite 103
Providence, RI 02903-1034
Phone: (401) 222-3880
Fax: (401) 521-1351
Email: randy@risca.state.ri.us

South Carolina Arts Commission
1800 Gervais Street
Columbia SC 29201
Phone: (803) 734-8696
Fax: (803) 734-8526
Email: surkamsu@arts.state.sc.us

South Dakota Arts Council
Office of the Arts
800 Governors Drive
Pierre, SD 57501-2294
Phone: (605) 773-3131
Fax: (605) 773-6962
Email: sdac@stlib.state.sd.us

Tennessee Arts Commission
Citizens Plaza
401 Charlotte Avenue
Nashville, TN 37243-0780
Phone: (615) 741-1701
Fax: (615) 741-8559
Email: btarleton@mail.state.tn.us

Texas Commission on the Arts
P.O. Box 13406, Capitol Station
Austin, TX 78711
Phone: (512) 463-5535
Fax: (512) 475-2699
Email: front.desk@arts.state.tx.us

Utah Arts Council
617 E. South Temple Street
Salt Lake City, UT 84102
Phone: (801) 236-7555
Fax: (810) 236-7556
Email: bstephen@arts.state.ut.us

Vermont Arts Council
136 State Street, Drawer 33
Montpelier, VT 05633-6001
Phone: (802) 828-3291
Fax: (802) 828-3363
Email: info@arts.vca.state.vt.us

Virgin Islands Council on the Arts
41-42 Norre Gade
P.O. box 103
St. Thomas, VI 00804
Phone: (340) 774-5984
Fax: (340) 774-6206

Virginia Commission for the Arts
223 Governor Street, 2nd Floor
Richmond, VA 23219
Phone: (804) 225-3132
Fax: (804) 225-4327
Email: vacomm.artswire.org

Washington State Arts Commission
P.O. Box 42675
Olympia, WA 98504-2675
Phone: (360) 753-3860
Fax: (360) 586-5351
Email: billp@wsac.wa.gov

West Virginia Commission on the Arts
1900 Kanawha Boulevard East
Charleston, WV 25305
Phone: (304) 558-0240
Fax: (304) 558-2779
Email: cook_1_r@wvlc.wvnet.edu

Wisconsin Arts Board
101 East Wilson Street, 1st Floor
Madison, WI 53702
Phone: (608) 266-0190
Fax: (608) 267-0380
Email: rtertin@arts.state.wi.us

Wyoming Arts Council
2320 Capitol Avenue
Cheyenne, WY 82002
Phone: (307) 777-7742
Fax: (307) 777-5499
Email: wyoarts@artswire.org

• • • •

"I love what I do and that is to help seniors do what they do best—entertain! I have no desire to ever be on stage—I'm just happy doing anything behind the scenes. It has been a wonderful and exciting time of life!"

Rosemarie Hannahs has spent ten years working backstage with the Oregon and the Northwest Senior Theatre as stage manager, assistant director, rehearsal pianist, and now is loving every minute of running the sound system!

REGIONAL ARTS ORGANIZATIONS

Arts Midwest
(IL, IN, IA, MI, MN, ND, OH, SD, WI)
Hennepin Center for the Arts
528 Hennepin Avenue, Suite 310
Minneapolis, MN 55403
Phone: (612) 341-0755
Fax: (612) 341-0902
Email: general@artsmidwest.org

Consortium for Pacific Arts and Cultures
(AS, CM, GU)
1580 Makaloa Street, Suite 930
Honolulu, HI 96814-3220
Phone: (808) 946-7381
Fax: (808) 955-2722
Email: cpac@pixi.com

Mid-America Arts Alliance
(AR, KS, MO, NE, OK, TX)
912 Baltimore Avenue, Suite 700
Kansas City, MO 64105
Phone: (816) 421-1388
Fax: (816) 421-3918

Mid-Atlantic Arts Foundation
(DE, DC, MD, NJ, NY, PA, VI, VA, WV)
22 Light Street, Suite 300
Baltimore, MD 21202
Phone: (410) 539-6656
Fax: (410) 837-5517
Email: maaf@midarts.usa.com

New England Foundation for the Arts
(CT, ME, MA, NH, RI, VT)
330 Congress Street, 6th Floor
Boston, MA 02210-1216
Phone: (617) 951-0010
Fax: (617) 951-0016
Email: info@nefa.org

Southern Arts Federation
(AL, FL, GA, KY, LA, MS, NC, SC, TN)
181 14th Street, N.E., Suite 400
Atlanta, GA 30309-7603
Phone: (404) 874-7244
Fax: (404) 873-2148

Western State Arts Federation

(AK, AZ, CA, CO, HI, ID, MT, MN, NV, OR, UT, WA, WY)
1543 Champa, Suite 220
Denver, CO 80202
Phone: (303) 629-1166
Fax: (303) 629-9717
Email: staff@westaf.org
Website: www.westaf.org

• • • •

"Being a member of the *Oregon Senior Theatre* for nine years was one of the most interesting and rewarding experiences of my life. At a time when many seniors are opting for less active roles, our theatre group was a heads-up, spirited company of zestful go-ers and do-ers. Our director inspired, coaxed, and demanded our best and we gave it to her. As a consequence, we were a successful organization, never lacking for bookings.

Aside from the satisfaction of giving pleasure to our audiences, fringe benefits for me were lasting friendships from diverse backgrounds, discovering abilities I didn't know I possessed, getting a close-up view of the film industry when I worked in movies and commercials, and traveling to many states I probably wouldn't have otherwise visited.

We went by bus, plane, car and never complained about schedules demanding dawn's early light departures or midnight's red-eyed returns. Theatre people are a special breed – optimistic, positive, flexible, with a never failing sense of humor. I treasure my years with the Oregon Senior Theatre."

Scotty Haskell

BIBLIOGRAPHY OF BOOKS, PLAY ANTHOLOGIES & ARTICLES

BOOKS

<u>Art in Other Places: Artists at Work in America's Community and Social Institutions.</u> Westport, CT: Praeger Publishers, 1992.

Basting, Anne Davis. <u>Stages of Age: Performing Age in Contemporary American Culture.</u> Ann Arbor, MI: University of Michigan Press, 1998.

Bertman, Sandra L. <u>Grief and the Healing Arts: Creativity and Therapy.</u> Amityville, NY: Baywood Publishing, 1999.

<u>Bibliography of Children's Books about Grandparents.</u> Oakland, CA: Stagebridge.

Boal, Augusto. <u>Games for Actors and Non-Actors.</u> New York: Rutledge Press, 1993.

Booth, Wayne. <u>The Art of Growing Older: Writers on Living and Aging.</u> Chicago, IL: University of Chicago Press, 1996.

Bornat, Joanna. <u>Reminiscence Reviewed: Perspectives, Evaluations, Achievements.</u> Buckingham, England: Open University Press, 1994.

Burger, Isabel. <u>Creative Drama for Senior Adults.</u> Connecticut: Morehouse Barlow Publishing Company, 1980.

Burnside, Irene. <u>Working with the Elderly: Group Processes and Techniques.</u> Belmont, CA: Wadsworth Publishing, 1978.

Cattanach, Ann. <u>Drama for People with Special Needs.</u> New York: Drama Publishers, 1996.

Chayefsky, Terry. <u>Acting in Prime Time: The Mature Person's Guide to Breaking into Show Business</u>. Westport, CT: Heinemann Trade Books, 1996.

Chopra, Deepak. <u>Ageless Body, Timeless Mind: The Quantum Alternative to Growing Old.</u> Three Rivers Press, 1998.

Clark, Patricia A. and Nancy J. Osgood. <u>Seniors on Stage: The Impact of Applying Theatre Techniques on the Elderly.</u> Praeger Publishing, 1985.

Cornish, Roger and Roger Kase, Editors. <u>Senior Adult Theatre.</u> University Park, Pennsylvania: Pennsylvania State University Press, 1981.

Dryden, Bob. <u>Staging A Snazzy Senior Showcase.</u> Brainerd, MN: Brainerd Community College, 1990.

Dyctwald, Kenneth. <u>Age Wave: How the Most Important Trend of Our Time Will Change Our Future.</u> Bantam Doubleday Dell, 1990.

Flatten, Kay. <u>Recreation Activities for the Elderly.</u> Springer Series on Adulthood and Aging, Volume 20, 1988.

Friedan, Betty. <u>The Fountain of Age.</u> New York: Simon and Schuster, 1993.

Gray, Paula. <u>Dramatics for the Elderly: A Guide for Residential Care Settings and Senior Centers.</u> New York: Columbia University Press, 1974.

Greenblatt, Fred S. <u>Drama with the Elderly: Acting At Eighty.</u> Charles C. Thomas Press, 1985.

Hart, Joan. <u>Beyond the Tunnel: The Arts and Aging in America.</u> Washington D.C.: Museum One Publications, 1992.

Hoffman, Donald H. <u>Arts for Older Americans: An Enhancement of Life.</u> Englewood Cliffs, NJ: Prentice Hall, 1991.

Jesse, Anita. <u>Let the Part Play You.</u> Burbank, CA: Wolf Creek Press, 1998.

Jesse, Anita. <u>The Playing is the Thing. Learning the Art of Aging Through Games and Exercise.</u> Burbank, CA: Wolf Creek Press, 1996.

Kaminsky, Marc. <u>The Uses of Reminiscence.</u> New York: Haworth Press, 1984.

Kastenbaum, Robert. <u>Defining Acts: Aging as Drama.</u> Amityville, NY: Baywood Publishing, 1994.

Koch, Kenneth. <u>I Never Told Anybody: Teaching Poetry in a Nursing Home.</u> New York: Random House, 1997.

Lamdin, Lois S. and Mary Connolly Fugate. <u>Elderlearning: New Frontiers in an Aging Society.</u> American Council on Education: Oryx Press Series on Higher Education, 1997.

Manheimer, Ronald J. <u>The Critical Condition of Arts and Humanities Programs for Older Adults.</u> American Society on Aging Workshop Presentation, 1998.

Manheimer, Ronald J. <u>The Arts and Humanities in an Aging Society: A Window of Opportunity in the Coming Decades.</u> Washington D.C.: The Presidents Committee on the Arts and Humanities, 1997.

Martz, Sandra Haldeman. <u>I Shall Wear Purple.</u> Paper Maché Press, 1991.

McCutcheon, Priscilla. <u>Developing Older Audiences: Guidelines for Performing Arts Groups.</u> Washington D.C.: National Council on the Aging, 1985.

McDonough, Ann. <u>The Golden Stage: Dramatic Activities for Older Adults.</u> Woodstock, IL: Dramatic Publishing, 1994.

McDonough, Ann. <u>The Golden Stage Instructor's Guide.</u> Woodstock, IL: Dramatic Publishing, 1994.

McLaren, Jean and Heidi Brown. <u>The Raging Grannies Songbook.</u> Gabriola Island, BC Canada: New Society Publishers.

McLeish, John A.B. <u>Creativity in the Later Years: An Annotated Bibliography.</u> New York: Garland Publishing, 1992.

McMurray, Janice. <u>Creative Arts with Older People.</u> Binghamton, NY: Haworth Press, 1990.

Myerhoff, Barbara. <u>Remembered Lives: The Work of Ritual, Storytelling and Growing Older.</u> Ed. Marc Kaminski. Ann Arbor, MI: University of Michigan Press, 1992.

National Assembly of State Arts Agencies, and the NEA. <u>Design for Accessibility: An Arts Administrators Guide.</u> Washington D.C., 1994.

National Council on the Aging. <u>Arts and Aging: An Agenda for Action.</u> Washington D.C., 1976.

Perlstein, Susan with Jeff Bliss. <u>Generating Community: Intergenerational Partnerships Through the Expressive Arts.</u> Brooklyn, NY: Elders Share the Arts, 1994.

Schaffner, Gertrude and Richard Courtney, Editors. <u>Drama in Therapy.</u> New York: Drama Book Specialists, 1979.

Schaffner, Gertrude and Richard Courtney, Editors. <u>Drama in Therapy Volume 2, Adults.</u> New York: Drama Book Specialists, 1981.

Serrano, Nina. <u>Pass it On: A Step by Step Manual for Developing A Volunteer Senior Storytelling in the Schools Program.</u> Oakland, CA: Stagebridge, 1999.

Singer, Dana. <u>Stage Writers Handbook: A Complete Business Guide for Playwrights, Composers, Lyricists and Librettists.</u> New York, NY: TCG Books, 1998.

Spencer, Michael Jon. <u>Live Arts Experiences: Their Impact on Health and Wellness.</u> New York, NY: Hospital Audiences, Inc., 1998.

Sunderland, Jacqueline. <u>Older Americans and the Arts: A Human Equation.</u> National Council on the Aging and the John F. Kennedy Center for the Performing Arts, 1974.

Telander, Marcie, Flora Quinalan, and Karol Verson. <u>Acting Up! An Innovative Approach to Creative Drama for Older Adults.</u> Woodstock, IL: Dramatic Publishing, 1982.

Thurman, Anne and Carol Ann Piggins. <u>Drama Activities with Older Adults: A Handbook for Leaders.</u> New York, NY: Haworth Press, 1982.

Vorenberg, Bonnie L. <u>A Guide to 49 New Plays for Senior Adult Theatre.</u> Portland, OR: Arts for Elders, 1985.

Vorenberg, Bonnie L. <u>Enriching and Older Person's Life Through Senior Adult Theatre.</u> Portland, OR: Arts for Elders, 1979.

Weisberg, Naida and Rosilyn Wilder. <u>Come, Step Into My Life: Youth and Elders Inter-Act.</u> Virginia: New Plays-Books, 1996.

Weisberg, Naida and Rosilyn Wilder. <u>Creative Arts with Older Adults.</u> Plenum Publishers, 1984.

Weisberg, Naida and Rosilyn Wilder. <u>Drama Therapy for Older Adults.</u> New Haven, CT: National Association for Drama Therapy, 1986.

Weisberg, Naida and Rosilyn Wilder. <u>The Lifestory of Re-Play Circle.</u> Pennsylvania: Venture Publishers, 1997.

PLAY ANTHOLOGIES

Abrams, Jules. <u>10 Senior Adult One Act Plays for Readers Theatre.</u> Return Engagement Press, 1999.

<u>Almost Anything for a Laugh.</u> Madison, WI: Bi-Folkal Productions, 1997.

<u>Almost Anything for a Laugh, Too.</u> Madison, WI: Bi-Folkal Productions, 1991.

<u>An Evening of One Act Stagers for Golden Agers.</u> New York: Samuel French, 1972.

Blanton, Gail. <u>Seniors Centerstage: 25 Sketch Scripts for Older Adults.</u> Kansas City, MO: Lillenas Publishing, 1998.

Cohen, Lorraine and Dr. Richard Imundo. <u>Scenes for Mature Actors</u>. Avon Books, 1998.

Cornish, Roger. <u>Short Plays for the Long Living.</u> Boston, MA: Baker's Plays, 1976.

Fuller, Ted. <u>Seniors Acting Up.</u> Pleasant Hill, CA: Pleasant Hill Press, 1996.

McDonough, Ann, Ed. <u>New Monologues for Mature Actors.</u> Woodstock, IL: Dramatic Publishing, 1997.

McDonough, Ann, Ed. <u>Short Stuff: Ten to Twenty Minute Plays for Senior Theatre.</u> Woodstock, IL: Dramatic Publishing, 1998.

Redd, Robert. <u>21 Humorous, New Short Plays and Skits for Performing Grandparents.</u> Ada, MI: Thornapple Publishing Company, 1998.

Spector, Linda. <u>Plays for Young and Old.</u> Oakland, CA: Stagebridge.

Vorenberg, Bonnie L. <u>New Plays for Mature Actors.</u> Woodstock, IL: Dramatic Publishing, 1986.

ARTICLES

"Aged to Perfection: The Amazing Theatre." Stage Directions. February, 1997: 17.

Baker, Beth. "Open to Revelation." Common Boundary. Sept/Oct., 1998.

Cornish, Roger. "Senior Adult Theatre--The State of the Art and a Call for Research." Theatre News. May, 1978.

"Drama Down at the Day Centre." New Age Concern Today. Spring, 1978: 25.

"Evergreen Theater." Stage Directions. April, 1990: 3.

"Full Service Theater: The Market House Theater." Stage Directions. February, 1996: 28.

"Getting Started in Senior Adult Theatre." Stage Directions. June, 1994: 8.

Henderson, Sallirae. "Choices in Dying: Senior Drama Group Explores End-of-Life Issue." Oregon's Journal on Aging. Fall, 1994. 8.

Hirsch, Amy. "Never Too Late: A Status Report on Senior Performers." Backstage Newspaper. August 28, 1992.

"It's Never Too Late to Act." Stage Directions. August, 1993: 1.

"It's SRO in New Mexico." Stage Directions. April, 1998: 14.

Kandall, Stewart. "Drama Emotion, Senior Citizens." California English. November, 1978.

Middleton, David and Kevin Buchanan. "Is Reminiscence Working? Accounting for the Therapeutic Benefits of Reminiscence Work with Older People." Journal of Aging Studies. 3 (1993): 321-33.

Nolter, M. "Drama for the Elderly: They Can Do It." Gerontologist. 2 (1973): 153-56.

Oatman, Eric. "Live Theatre is Alive and Well...With a Role for You." Retirement Living. December, 1975: 27-29.

Performances for the Elderly or Handicapped." Stage Directions. June, 1990: 6.

ARTICLES *(Continued)*

Pearson, Susan. "Drama with Senior Adults: Breaking the Ice." <u>Children's Theatre Review,</u> Volume 28, No. 4.

Phlanzer, Howard. "Older People Act Up: Making the Ordinary Extraordinary." <u>TDR.</u> Spring, 1992: 115-23.

Provus, Birdell and Karol Verson. "Acting Up! Knocks Down Sterotypes." <u>Perspective on Aging</u>. January/February, 1986: 8.

Smith, Nancy. "New Wrinkle Theatre: Drama Drawn from Experience." <u>New Age.</u> February, 1979: 48-9.

Stretar, Joseph. "Community Colleges and the Educational Needs of Older Adults." <u>The Education Digest.</u> April, 1975: 28-30.

Tarzian, Pat. "Taking Up Acting At the Ripe Age of Sixty Plus." <u>Montclarion.</u> April, 1979.

Vorenberg, Bonnie L. "Drama in a Supportive Environment: It's More Than Just a Play." <u>GeriActive Exchange.</u> November, December, 1983.

Vorenberg, Bonnie L. "Stimu-Drama: An Eclectic Approach." <u>Senior Adult Program Bulletin.</u> Children's Theatre Association of America. December 5, 1980.

GENERAL

A.A.U.W. Readers Theatre 7
Abrams, Jules 24, 51, 113
Academy Theatre 7
Acting in Prime Time 81
Adamson, Jo J. 51
Adler, Jeff 20
Age Exchange Theatre and Reminiscence Centre 37
Aida 39
Alabama State Council on the Arts 96
Alaska State Council on the Arts 96
Alicea, Amy 21
Allan Lotsberg's NEW Fogey Follies 7
American Association of Community Theatre 83, 86
American Council on Education 110
American Samoa Council on Culture,
    Arts and Humanities 96
American Society on Aging (ASA) 83, 110
Americans for the Arts 83
Amlia Community Theatre 75
Anchorage Community Theatre, Inc. 75
Anchorage Press, Inc. 52, 61
Anderson Senior Follies 8
Angelo, Julie 83
Anthony, Cynthia 80
Apple Valley Players 7
Ariza, Señora Patricia 39
Arizona Commission on the Arts 96
Arkansas Arts Council 96
Arlington Friends of the Drama, Inc. 75
Armory Square Playhouse 51
Armstrong, Kay 79
Art Age Publications 22, 45, 64
Articles About Senior Theatre 114
Arts and Healing Network 83
Arts for All 47
Arts for Elders 112
Arts Funding 95
Arts Midwest 106
Asheville Community Theatre 75
Association for Gerontology in Higher Education 83
Association for Theatre and Disability 83
Association for Theatre in Higher Education 85
Ault, Charles J. 47
Austin, Deborah R. 7, 75
Austin Scriptworks 52
Autumn Players, The 7

Back Porch Dance Company 7
Backstage Newspaper 114
Bagnole, Joe 77
Baker, Beth 114

Baker, Dr. Robert 24
Baker's Plays 52, 113
Bantam Doubleday Dell 110
Barker, Richard 80
Barnes, Wendell 47
Basting, Anne Davis 47, 109
Bastrop Opera House 75
Bay City Players, Inc. 75
Baywood Publishing 107, 109, 110
Belfry Players 75
Bell, Beverly 81
Beller, Jonathan 80
Bengston, Paul 78
Benton, Bill 52
Bertman, Sandra L. 109
Berzau, Ingrid 41
Better Than Ever Independents, Inc. 7
Bevilacqua, Silvia 39, 40
Bi-Folkal Productions 53, 113
Biasutti, Loretta 34
Binko, Virginia 33
Bittner, Eva 42
Black, F. Scott 76
Blanton, Gail 113
Bliss, Jeff 111
Boal, Augusto 109
Bogan, Linda 11
Boise Actors' Guild 75
Bonner, Kirsten 24
Books 109
Booth, Wayne 109
Born, Walter L. 76
Bornat, Joanna 109
Brainerd Community College 110
Brant, Eric 76
Bray, Michael 81
Brevard Little Theatre 75
Bridges, Shirley 11
Brightwell, Betty 34
Britt, Mary 79
Broadway Academy of Performing Arts 25
Brown, Beverly 28
Brown, Heidi 111
Brown University 47
Bryan, Victoria 72
Buchanan, Kevin 114
Buker, Newt 32
Burgen, Chuck 32
Burger, Isabel 109
Burnham, Bob 20

Burnside, Irene 109
Business of Writing for the Theatre 50
Byrne, Mrs. J.M. 77

C.A.S.T. 75
California Arts Council 97
California English 114
Calvert City Office on Aging 32
Camargo, Beatriz 42
Campell Stemple, Beth 59
Carvajal, Joseph J. 75
Cattanach, Ann 109
Cecia 75
Cedar Falls Community Theatre 76
Charles C. Thomas Press 110
Charleston Working Theatre, Inc. 76
Chase, Murray 81
Chatham Community Players 76
Chayefsky, Terry 81, 109
Cheneaux, Monsieur Rene 40
Cherry, Al 45
Cheyenne Little Theatre Players 76
Chiedza Theater Group 39
Children's Theatre Review 114
Chin, John 54
Chin, Kimberly 54
Chiweshe Reich, Ambuya Stella 39
Chopra, Deepak 109
Chronical of Philanthropy, The 95
Chula Vista Senior Citizen Club 11
Cilman, Bob 32
Clark, Patricia A. 109
Class Act, The 10
Cloud, Cindy 78
Cochran, Michael 78
Cockpit in Court Summer Theatre 76
Coelho, Fernanda 39
Coffman, Dr. Victoria 47, 66
Coghill, Joy 35
Cohen, Harold 20, 54, 57
Cohen, Lorraine 113
Cohen, Mrs. Jessica 39
Colorado Council of the Arts 97
Columbia University Press 110
Commonwealth Council for Arts and Culture 102
Communi-Culture Performing Arts Association 11
Community Access to the Arts 11
Community Actors of Saint Bernard 76
Community Light Opera and Theatre 76
Community Theatre Guild, Inc. 76
Community Theatre League 76

Concord Senior Citizens Club 11
Connecticut Commission on the Arts 97
Connolly Fugate, Mary 110
Consortium for Pacific Arts and Cultures 106
Corbett, Donna 79
Corbin, Sister Germaine 13
Cornish, Roger 110, 113, 114
Corporacion Colombiana de Teatro 39
Courtney, Richard 111
Cradle to Grave Arts 11
Creative Drama Magazine 68
Creative Productions, Inc. 76
Crosser, Dennis 17
Culver City Senior Center 11
Currier, Lesley S. 78
Curtain Time Players 11
Curtain Time Retirement Vignettes 11

Dance Generators, The 11
Dance Wheels 11
Danville Light Opera 76
Decker, Angela 71
Delaware Division of the Arts 97
DeLuna, Jan 20
Dennison, Hannah 11
Denolf, Mary Jo 11
Denver Civic Theatre 76
Department of the Army Music & Theatre 76
Detroit Theatre Organ Society 76
Detwiler, Lendl 77
Die WellenbrecherDie/Wagemutigen/Altentheaterwerks 39
DiMurro, Terry 80
District of Columbia Commission on the Arts and Humanities 98
Dolmieu, Dominique 40
Dow, Janet H. 59
Dowling, Amie 11
Down, Susan 78
Downtown Drama Company 76
Drama Book Specialists 111
Drama Dears 11
Drama Publishers 109
Dramata Editions 68
Dramatic Publishing 54, 55, 111, 112, 115
Dryden, Bob 110
Dudley Riggs Creative Services 76
Dupree, Elizabeth 21
Dyctwald, Kenneth 110

East Essex Players 77
Education Digest, The 115
Educational Theatre Association 83, 84
Eitze, Chester 75
Elborne, Francis W. 80
Elderhostel 68
Elders Share the Arts (ESTA) 22, 50, 71, 73, 87, 111
Elements, The 39
Encore Performance Publishing 56
Encore Theatre 12
Enter Laughing, Inc. 77
Entertainers, The 11
Epilogue Players 77
Epstein, Annette Cantrell 9, 48, 56
Erreca, Wayne Alan 79
Ewing, Craig 80
Extended Run Players 13
Extension Dance Studio 21

Fab Fifties Follies, The 17
Fabulous Palm Spring Follies 14
Fanlight Productions 87
Fargo-Morehead Community Theatre 77
FATE Productions 77
Fernandina Little Theatre 77
FestivAge 39
Fey, Lorenne 7
Fick, Señora Guillermina 40
Filmakers Library 88
Finnerty, Joseph J. 56
First Avenue Playhouse-Starburst 77
Fitzpatrick, Marlene 78
Flatten, Kay 110
Flint Community Players, Inc. 77
Florida Division of Cultural Affairs 98
Footnotes, The 34
Footsteps of the Elders 15, 50
Ford Center, The 7
Forsha, Diana 77
Fort Smith Little Theatre 77
Fort Wayne Civic Theatre, Inc. 77
Foti, Sonda 77
Foundation Center, The 94
Foundations On-Line 95
Fountain Valley Seniors 17
Fourth of July Creek Productions 77
Foxettes RiverCity Theater -
    Silver Foxettes and the Guys 17
Francis, Betty J. 25
Franklin, Al 77
French, Samuel 113

Friedl, Eckhard 42
Friedan, Betty 110
Frisco Community Theatre 77
Fugate, Mary Connolly 110
Full Circle Theatre 17
Fuller, Ted 29, 59, 61, 113
Funsters, The 17
Furlan, Kris 23, 79

Gant Oninski, Angie 79
Garland Publishing 111
Gaslight Theatre 77
Generationstheater Artemis 39
Gaydos, Thomas V. 47
Georgia Council for the Arts 98
GeriActive Exchange 115
Geritol Follies, The 34
Geritol Frolics 17
Gerontologist 114
Gershuny, Lee 39
Godiciu, Debra 80
Golden Troupers Readers Theatre And Singers, The 20
"Gotta Dance!" Entertainment Troupe 20
Gowen, M. Charline 47
Grand Generation Center 50
Grand Opera House 77
Grandparents Living Theatre 18
Grant Getter's Guide to the Internet 95
Grant Writing and Fund Raising Information Resources 95
Grants Information Center, The 95
Grantsmanship Center, The 94
Gray, Frank 32
Gray, Paula 110
Greater Grand Forks Community Theatre 77
Green, Carole K. 75
Green Earth Players 77
Green, Joan 7
Greenblatt, Fred S. 110
Greene Shaffer, Myra 77
Greenwood Community Theatre 77
Groupo Fraternidad 40
Grupo de Teatro Nucleo 1 39
Grupo de Terceira Edade 39
Guam Council on the Arts and Humanities 98
Gustafson, Jim 56

Haarbauer, Martha 26
Hake, Dorothy 34
Hamilton, Chris 34
Hamilton City Lights 33
Handel, Judie 75

Hannahs, Rosemarie 105
Harbor Playhouse 78
Harden, Vern 7, 57
Hart, Joan 110
Hart, Kate 77
Haschke, Nicki E. 79
Hashagen, Werner 58
Haskell, Scotty 108
Hauppauge Players, The 20
Hawaii Foundation on Culture and the Arts 98
Haworth Press 110, 111, 112
Heart of the Matter Productions 58
Heinemann 81
Heinemann Trade Books 109
Heinich, Angelika 39
Henderson, Imogene 67
Henderson, Nancy 76
Henderson, Sallirae 114
Hennessy, Richard 76
Heptner, Joyce 79
Hertz, Bill 76
Highland Senior Players 20
Hirsch, Amy 114
Hoffman, Donald H. 110
Hook, Cora 32
Hoover, Pat S. 78
Horizon Senior Ensemble 20
Hornsveld, Frau Ingeborg 42
Hospital Audiences, Inc. 45, 112
Hruby, Norbert 58
Hudack, Nancy 78
Hull, Daphne R. 58
Huntington Playhouse 78
Hurst, Walter K. 78
Hutter, Rob 17
Hymittos Theatre 40

!Improvise! Inc. 50
I.E. Clark Publications 54
Ice House Theatre 78
Ichabod's Little Theatre in the Hollow 78
Idaho Commission on the Arts 98
Impact 40
Illinois Arts Council 98
Illinois Theatre Association 78
Imagination Power Company, The 47
Imundo, Dr. Richard 113
Independent Sector 94
Indiana Arts Commission 99
Institute for Readers Theatre 68, 69

International Federation on Ageing 83
Institute for Therapy Through the Acts, The 70
Institute of Puerto Rican Culture 103
International Arts Medicine Association 83
Internet Nonprofit Center 95
Iowa Arts Council 99

Jameson, James & Bronwyn 58
Jardin, Dan 14
Jaspers, Carleen 58
Jelinek, Lynnette 21
Jenkins, Margaret D. 22
Jenks, Don 76
Jeriatric Jubilee 21
Jesse, Anita 110
Joao Henrique Bernardi, Londrina 39
John F. Kennedy Center for the Performing Arts 112
Johnson City Community Theatre 78
Johnson, Kristin 76
Johnson, Nancy 78
Johnson, P. Anna 24
Jones, Charles B. 78
Jones, Don 11
Jones, John T. 75
Jones, Walton 77
Joplin Little Theatre 78
Journal of Aging Studies 114
Just Gotta Tap 21

Kaiser, Johanna 42
Kalinska, Zofia 39
Kaminsky, Janice 88
Kaminsky, Marc 110, 111
Kandall, Stewart 31, 114
Kansas Arts Commission 99
Kase, Roger 110
Kastenbaum, Robert 110
Kenneth Scott Vocal Theatre, Inc. 78
Kentucky Arts Council 99
Kershaw, Ruth 40
Kick Theatre 40
Kids on the Block, Inc., The 21
Kingner, Günter 42
Koch, Kenneth 110
Korner, Barbara O. 43
Kyle, Evelyn 7

LaBrie, John 68, 69
Lafoon, Don 72
LaFleche, Don 83
Lakeland Cultural Arts Center 78

Lamberson, Dennis 17
Lamdin, Lois S. 110
Lane, Dawn 47
Largo Cultural Center 78
Late Edition, The 22
Le Chaix, Barbara 11
Le Mars Community Theatre 78
Le Volontariat au Service de l'Art 40
Lekas, Gerry 58
Leonard, Geoff D. 79
Lerman, Liz 47
L'Espace d'un Instant 40
Letsche, Jayne 28
Lindquist, Arne 27
Little Theatre of Monroe, Inc. 78
Little Town Players 78
Liz Lerman Dance Exchange 22
Loeffler, Don 47
Lord Chilton, Peggy 25
Lorenzetti, Diane 11
Louisiana Division of the Arts 99
Lowenstein, Henry 76
Luzaich, John C. 76
Lyman, Vivian 22

Madorin, Charlotte 42
MacÐougal, P. Paullette 52
Maine Arts Commission 99
Manatee Players 78
Manfred, Fred 77
Manheimer, Ronald J. 110, 111
Mardiros, Betty 34
Margolis, Kari 85
Marin Shakespeare Company 78
Market House Theatre 78
Martins Pedrao, Alyson 39
Maryland State Arts Council 100
Martz, Sandra Haldeman 111
Marziali, Maria Teresa 40
Mass. Cultural Council Elder Arts Initiative 50
Massachusetts Cultural Council 100
Mathews, Marguerite 23
Mature Talent Enterprises 67
Matzke, Frank 42
Maurice, Rosemarie 34
Mavroudi, Cleo 40
McBride, Donna 78
McClane, Linda 75
McCrory, Sue 22
McCutcheon, Priscilla 111
McDonough, Dr. Ann 47, 66, 111, 113, 115

MacDougal, P. Paullette 52
McLaren, Jean 111
McLeish, John A.B. 111
McMurray, Janice 111
Melbourne Civic Theatre 78
Meren, John 79
Meridian Little Theatre 79
Merry Clements Players 22
Meszaros, Edward 80
Meyrose, Tom 78
Michigan Council for Arts and Cultural Affairs 100
Mid-America Arts Alliance 106
Mid-Atlantic Arts Foundation 106
Middleton, David 114
Minnesota State Arts Board 100
Mira Theatre Guild 79
Misko-Coury, Lillian 23, 47
Mississippi Arts Commission 100
Missouri Arts Council 100
Mokofsky, Steven 77
Montana Arts Council 101
Montana State University 47, 66
Montclarion 115
Mooresville Senior Center 22
Mordaunt, Ninette S. 32
Morehouse Barlow Publishing Company 109
Morrisson, Maggi 39
Mount Prospect Theatre Society 79
Mowatt, Don 35
Museum One Publications 110
Myerhoff, Barbara 111

Naples Players, Inc. 79
National Arts and Disability Center 50
National Assembly of State Arts Agencies, and the NEA 111
National Association for Drama Therapy (NADT) 85, 112
National Association for Poetry Therapy (APT) 85
National Coalition of Arts Therapies Association 85
National Council on the Aging 85, 86, 111, 112
National Endowment for the Arts 50, 95
National Movement Theatre Association 85
National Theatre Community Vaudeville 45
Nebraska Arts Council 101
Nein, Betsy 17
Nevada Arts Council 101
New Age 115
New Age Concern Today 114
New Castle Senior Activity Group 22
New England Foundation for the Arts 106
New England Theatre Conference 85

New Hampshire State Council on the Arts 101
New Jersey State Council on the Arts 101
New Mexico Arts 101
New Plays-Books 112
New Society Publishers 111
New Wrinkles Show 22
New York State Council on the Arts 102
Newman, Sandra 11
Nielsen, Larry 81
Nipper, Bennie 78
Nocks, Nancy S. 19
Nolter, M. 114
Nomads Theatre Workshop 79
North Carolina Arts Council 102
North Dakota Council on the Arts 102
Northeastern University 85
Northwest Senior Theatre 22

OASIS Institute, The 70
Oatman, Eric 114
Ocala Civic Theatre 79
Octad-One Productions, Inc. 79
Oestman, Randy 76
Off Washington Players 22
Ohio Arts Council 102
Ohio State University 49, 66, 89
Okhlopokov Drama Theatre 40
Oklahoma Arts Council 102
Oklahoma Community Theatre Association 79
Older People's Drama Group 40
Older Women's Network 40
Older Women's Theatre Group 40
Olendorf, Mary 78
Olivotto, Yolanda 36
Omansky, Adrienne 67
Open University Press 109
O'Regan, Phil 42
Oregon Arts Commission 103
Oregon Senior Theatre xi
Oregon's Journal on Aging 114
O'Reilly, Win 24, 32
Ormandy, Lynne 32
Oryx Press Series on Higher Education 110
Osgood, Nancy J. 109

Paiste, Terryl 58, 59
Paper Maché Press 112
Pappas, Anna 10
Paquette, Jerold J. 76
Pavlis, Ester R. 7
Pawloski, Jim 75
Pearls of Wisdom, The 22

Pearson, Susan 114
Pecker, Sara 24
PEN American Center 94
Peng, Ms. Ya-Ling 42
Penn State 47
Penn State Goldenaires 23
Pennell, Steven 29, 47
Pennsylvania Council on the Arts 103
Pennsylvania State University Press 110
Pensacola Little Theatre, Inc. 79
Peoples, Donna 79
Peoria Players Theatre 79
Performing Arts Society of Nevada 79
Perkins, Mike 80
Perlstein, Susan 22, 50, 71, 111
Perron, Dr. Dorothy 24
Perry, Michael 32
Perry, Mike 56
Perspectives on Aging 115
Philanthropy Journal Online 95
Phillips, Andree 76
Phlanzer, Howard 115
Pierce, Ruth S. 50
Pigford, Jummy 79
Piggins, Carol Ann 112
Pinkman, Sue 79
Pioneer Drama Service 58, 60
Play Anthologies 113
Players Guild of Canton, The 23, 79
Player's Guild of the Festival Playhouse 47
Playwrights Anonymous 59
Pleasant Hill Press 59, 61, 113
Plenum Publishers 112
Polaris 95
Poloma, Jude 76
Pontine Theatre 23
Popular Play Service 59
Port Ludlow Players 24
Praeger Publishers 109
Prime Time Players 24
Prentice Hall 110
Prescott, Robert 78
Presidents Committee on the Arts and Humanities, The 111
Primus Theatre 24
Provus, Birdell 115

Quannapowitt Players 79
Queens Senior Safety Theatre Troupe 24
Quinalan, Flora 112
Quincy Community Theatre 24, 79

Raging Grannies of Calgary 34
Raging Grannies of Edmonton 34
Raging Grannies of Seattle, The 24
Raging Grannies of Victoria 40
Rais, Paula 50
Raker, Elizabeth W. 75
Random House 110
Rayfeld, Sidy 17
Raynor, Ph.D., Olivia 50, 83
Read, Randall 32, 81
Readers Theatre Script Service 59, 69
Redd, Robert 11, 113
Reep, Allen 80
Reidel, Susan J. 77
Reilly, Dr. Joy 49, 66, 89
Reilly, Shannon 80
Reston Community Players 79
Retirement Living 114
Return Engagement Players 24
Return Engagement Plays 51, 51
Return Engagement Press 113
Rhode Island State Council on the Arts 103
Rhythmic Visions 34
Richards, Glenda 34
Richburn Entertainment 34
Richter, Cheryl 77
Riggs, Dudley 76
Ripley-Lotee, Deanna 76
River's Bend Playhouse, Inc. 79
Roaring Springs, Eliza 12
Robello, Nicoletta 42
Robert, Monsieur Christian 39
Roberts, Aileen 77
Robinson, Roslyn 22
Rockwall Community Playhouse 79
Rosen, Delores 80
Rothman Vojta, Barbara 11
Rowell, Barbara 24, 79
Rubenstein, Ted 70
Rutledge Press 109

Saari, Steve 77
Sage Players 24
Salas, Victor M. 32
San Luis Obispo Little Theatre 80
San Pedro Playhouse 80
Schaffner, Gertrude 111
Scholz, Dieter 41
Schuneman, Bernie 80
Schweitzer, Pam 38
Seasoned Performers, The 26
Seibert, Ed 46

Senior Adult Program Bulletin 115
Senior Barn Players 24
Senior Class, The 25
Senior Commercial Acting Program 67
Senior Ensemble of the Freies Werkstatt Theater Koln
    (Dachverband Altenkultur) 41
Senior Players of American River Community (SPARC) 25
Senior Resource Center, Inc. 32
Senior Star Showcase 27
Senior Theatre Connections 22, 50, 64
Senior Theatre Reseärch & Performance 85
Senior Theatre Scripts 57
Senior Ventures 71
Seniorentheater SeTa e.V 40
Seniorentheater Spatlese e. V 42
Seniors Acting Up 61
Seniors' Jubilee 34
Seniors Reaching Out 24
Serrano, Nina 111
Shannon, Chuck 20
Silver Wings Repertory Company 29
Simon and Schuster 110
Sims, Mozelle 67
Singer, Dana 50, 112
Singleton, Darlene 79
Sixty Karats 28
Slightly Older Adult Players (S.O.A.P.) 29
Small, Norman M. 80
Smith, Kathryn E. 44
Smith, Nancy 115
Smith, Wallace 78
Snippets Historical and Cultural Drama Group 42
Society for the Arts in Healthcare 85
Solomon, Victoria 7
South Carolina Arts Commission 103
South Dakota Arts Council 103
Southeast Focal Point Senior Center 32
Southern Arts Federation 106
Southern Oregon University 71
Southwest Playhouse Fine Arts Center 80
Spector, Linda 113
Spencer, Michael Jon 112
SPRI Theatre Company (Senior Players of Rhode Island) 29, 47
Springer Series on Adulthood and Aging 109
Stage & Screen Book Club 59, 62, 63
Stage Coach Players 80
Stage Crafters Community Theatre 80
Stage Directions 114
Stagebridge 30, 90, 109, 111, 112, 113
Staten Island Shakespearean Theatre Co. 80
Sterling Playmakers 80
Stewart, Doug 22, 50

Stienike, Lois 50
Still Acting Up! 32
Stoebling, Craig 80
STOP-GAP Institute, The 72
Streltsov, Anatoly 40
Stretar, Joseph 115
Stut Theater 42
Sunderland, Jacqueline 112

TCG Books 112
TDR 115
Tanztheater Dritter Frühling 42
Tarzian, Pat 115
Taylor, Melissa E. 79
Teatr Osrodek Stacja Szamocin 42
Teatro NACE (Nuevos Actores and Cultura Expresiva) 32
Telander, Marcie 112
Temple Civic Theatre 80
Tennessee Arts Commission 104
Terra Nova Films 91, 92
Terry, Paula 50
Texas Commission on the Arts 104
Theater Alt and Jung 42
Theater der Erfahrungen 42
Theater Mühleimer Spatlese 42
Theatre News 114
Theatergroep Delta 42
Theatre Cedar Rapids 80
Theatre Company of Rhode Island 80
Theatre in the Park 80
Theatre of Western Springs 80
Theatre Winterhaven 80
Theatre Works 80
Theatre Works' Golden Troupers 32
Theatrikos 80
Third Age Theatre Company 32
This Wide & Universal Theatre 59
Thomson, Julia 32, 80
Thornapple Publishing Company 113
Thornton Senior Center 22
Three Rivers Press 109
Thurber, Michael 80
Thurman, Anne 112
Tinker, Bruce 77
Toelke, Randy 79
Topeka Civic Theatre 80
Torchbearers 32
Touchstone Theatre 32
Township Center for the Performing Arts 80
Trumbull New Theatre 80
Türk-Chlapek, Ingrid 39
Twin Cities Players, Inc. 81

Uhan Shii Theatre 42
Universita III Eta 42
University of Chicago Press 109
University of Michigan Press 111
University of Nevada Las Vegas 47, 66
University of Southern Maine 68, 69
Utah Arts Council 104

Valley of the Stars Community Theatre 32, 81
van Kempen, Mr. Marcel 42
van Labeke, Silvain 40
Vanden Bosch, James 91
Vanevenhoven, Maxine 17
Variety Players 32
Venice Little Theatre 81
Venture Publishers 112
Vercken, Francoise 40
Vermont Arts Council 104
Verson, Karol 112, 115
Very Special Arts 85
Victoria Target Theatre Society 36
Victory Players 81
Village Players, Inc. 81
Vintage Players 32
Vintage Players of Provo Utah 32
Vintage Players, The 32
Virgin Islands Council on the Arts 104
Virginia Commission for the Arts 104
voor Ouderen Sima van, Keative Dans 42
Vorenberg, Bonnie L. v, 50, 112, 113, 115

Wadsworth Publishing 109
Waimea Community Theatre 81
Washington State Arts Commission 104
Weber, Art 22
Weisberg, Gloria 32
Weisberg, Naida D. 50, 112
Werk-en Studiengroep 42
West Virginia Commission on the Arts 105
Western Gold Theatre Society 35
Western State Arts Federation 107
Wilder, Rosilyn 50, 112
Wilkinson, Kate 90
Williams, Sandra 77
Wisconsin Arts Board 105
Wolf Creek Press 110
Worthington, Sarah 15, 50
Wright, Tom 22
Wrinkles of Washington 32
Wyoming Arts Council 105

Young at Heart Chorus 32

Zarembinska, Frau Luba 42

GEOGRAPHICAL

ALABAMA
Alabama State Council on the Arts 96
Seasoned Performers, The 26

ALASKA
Alaska State Council on the Arts 96
Anchorage Community Theatre, Inc. 75

ARIZONA
Arizona Commission on the Arts 96
Entertainers, The 11
Joseph J. Finnerty 56
Prime Time Players 18
Senior Class, The 25
Theatre Works 80
Theatre Works' Golden Troupers 32
Theatrikos 80

ARKANSAS
Arkansas Arts Council 96
Fort Smith Little Theatre 77
Village Players, Inc. 81

AUSTRIA
Generationstheater Artemis 39

BELGUIM
Impact 40

BRASIL
Grupo de Teatro Nucleo 1 39
Grupo de Terceira Edade 39

CALIFORNIA
American Society on Aging (ASA) 83
Arts and Healing Network 83
Association for Theatre and Disability 83
California Arts Council 97
Chin, Kimberly 54
Chula Vista Senior Citizen Club 11
Community Light Opera and Theatre 76
Concord Senior Citizens Club 11
Culver City Senior Center 11
Fabulous Palm Spring Follies 14
Fourth of July Creek Productions 77
Funsters, The 17
Grantsmanship Center, The 94
Hashagen, Werner 58
Institute for Readers Theatre 68
Marin Shakespeare Company 78
Mira Theatre Guild 79

National Arts and Disability Center 50
New Wrinkles Show 22
Octad-One Productions, Inc. 79
Pleasant Hill Press 59, 113
Readers Theatre Scripts Service 59
San Luis Obispo Little Theatre 80
Senior Commercial Acting Program 67
Senior Players of American River Community (SPARC) 25
Silver Wings Repertory Company 29
Stagebridge 30, 90, 111, 112, 113
STOP-GAP Institute, The 72
Valley of the Stars Community Theatre 32, 81
Wadsworth Publishing 109
Wolf Creek Press 110

CANADA
Footnotes, The 34
Geritol Follies, The 34
Hamilton City Lights 33
International Federation on Ageing 83
New Society Publishers 111
Raging Grannies of Calgary 34
Raging Grannies of Edmonton 34
Raging Grannies of Victoria 34
Rhythmic Visions 34
Seniors' Jubilee 34
Victoria Target Theatre Society 36
Western Gold Theatre Society 35

COLORADO
A.A.U.W. Reader's Theatre 7
Apple Valley Players 7
Benton, Bill 52
Colorado Council of the Arts 97
Denver Civic Theatre 76
Fountain Valley Seniors 17
Highland Senior Players 20
Merry Clements Players 22
Off Washington Players 22
Pioneer Drama Service 58
Player's Guild of the Festival Playhouse 47
Senior Theatre Scripts by Vern Harden 57
Slightly Older Adult Players (S.O.A.P.) 29
Society for the Arts in Healthcare 85
Western State Arts Federation 107

COLUMBIA
Corporacion Colombiana de Teatro 39

CONNECTICUT
Campell Stemple, Beth 59
Connecticut Commission on the Arts 97
FATE Productions 77
Heinemann Trade Books 109
Morehouse Barlow Publishing Company 109
National Association for Drama Therapy 112
Popular Play Service 59
Praeger Publishers, 109

DELEWARE
Delaware Division of the Arts 97

ENGLAND
Age Exchange Theatre and Reminiscence Center 38
East Essex Players 77
Open University Press 109

FLORIDA
Amlia Community Theatre 75
Enter Laughing, Inc. 77
Fab Fifties Follies, The 17
Fernandina Little Theatre 77
Florida Division of Cultural Affairs 98
Gaydos, Thomas V. 47
Golden Troupers Readers Theatre And Singers, 20
"Gotta Dance!" Entertainment Troupe 20
Ice House Theatre 78
Just Gotta Tap 21
Largo Cultural Center 78
Manatee Players 78
Melbourne Civic Theatre 78
Naples Players, Inc. 79
Ocala Civic Theatre 79
Pensacola Little Theatre, Inc. 79
Southeast Focal Point Senior Center 32
Stage Crafters Community Theatre 80
Theatre Winterhaven 80
Township Center for the Performing Arts 80
Venice Little Theatre 81

FRANCE
FestivAge 39
Kick Theatre 40
Le Volontariat au Service de l'Art 40
L'Espace d'un Instant 40

GEORGIA
Academy Theatre 7
Arts for All 47
Georgia Council for the Arts 98

Horizon Senior Ensemble 20
Imagination Power Company, The 47

GERMANY
Die Wallenbrecher/Die Wagemutigen/Altentheat 39
Senior Ensemble of the Freies Werkstatt Th 41
Seniorentheater Spatlese e. V 42
Seniorentheater SeTA e. V 40
Theater Alt and Jung 42
Theater der Erfahrungen 42
Theater Muhleimer Spatlese 42

GREECE
Hymittos Theatre 40

GUAM
Guam Council on the Arts and Humanities 98

HAWAII
Consortium for Pacific Arts and Cultures 106
Hawaii Foundation on Culture and the Arts 98
Waimea Community Theatre 81

HOLLAND
Stut Theater 42
Theatergroep Delta 42
Werk-en Studiengroep 42

IOWA
Cedar Falls Community Theatre 76
Downtown Drama Company 76
Grand Opera House 77
Iowa Arts Council 99
Le Mars Community Theatre 78
Theatre Cedar Rapids 80

IDAHO
Boise Actors' Guild 75
Idaho Commission on the Arts 98

ILLINOIS
Danville Light Opera 76
Dramatic Publishing 54, 111, 112, 113
Illinois Arts Council 98
Illinois Theatre Association 78
Institute for Therapy Through the Acts, The 70
Jeriatric Jubilee 21
Jim Gustafson 56
Lekas, Gerry 58
Mount Prospect Theatre Society 79
Peoria Players Theatre 79

ILLINOIS (Continued)
Primus Theatre 24
Quincy Community Theatre 79
Quincy Community Theatre Silver Stars 24
Senior Theatre Research & Performance 85
Stage Coach Players 80
Still Acting Up! 32
Terra Nova Films 91
Theatre of Western Springs 80
University of Chicago Press 109

INDIANA
Community Theatre Guild, Inc. 76
Epilogue Players 77
Fort Wayne Civic Theatre, Inc. 77
Indiana Arts Commission 99
Mooresville Senior Center 22
River's Bend Playhouse, Inc. 79
Stage & Screen Book Club 59
Third Age Theatre Company 32
Vintage Players, The 32

IRELAND
Snippets Historical and Cultural Drama 42

ITALY
Aida 39
Older Women's Network 40
Older Women's Theatre Group 40
Universita III Eta 42

KANSAS
Kansas Arts Commission 99
Senior Barn Players 24
Topeka Civic Theatre 80

KENTUCKY
Kentucky Arts Council 99
Market House Theatre 78

LOUISIANA
Anchorage Press, Inc. 52
Community Actors of Saint Bernard 76
Little Theatre of Monroe, Inc. 78
Louisiana Division of the Arts 99

MAINE
Heart of the Matter Productions 58
Maine Arts Commission 99

MARYLAND
Class Act, The 10
Hull, Daphne R. 58
Kids on the Block, Inc., The 21
Liz Lerman Dance Exchange 22
Maryland State Arts Council 100
Mid-Atlantic Arts Foundation 106
Return Engagement Players 24
Return Engagement Plays 59
Senior Star Showcase 27
Variety Players 32

MASSACHUSETTS
Arlington Friends of the Drama, Inc. 75
Back Porch Dance Company 7
Baker's Plays 52
Charleston Working Theatre, Inc. 76
Dance Generators, The 11
Dance Wheels 11
Elderhostel 68
Fanlight Productions 88
Mass. Cultural Council Elder Arts Initiative 50
Massachusetts Cultural Council 100
New England Foundation for the Arts 106
New England Theatre Conference 85
Quannapowitt Players 79
Victory Players 81
Young at Heart Chorus 32

MICHIGAN
Bay City Players, Inc. 75
Curtain Time Players 11
Curtain Time Retirement Vignettes 11
Detroit Theatre Organ Society 76
Flint Community Players, Inc. 77
Hruby, Norbert 58
Ichabod's Little Theatre in the Hollow 78
Michigan Council for Arts and Cultural Affairs 100
Thornapple Publishing Co. 113
Twin Cities Players, Inc. 81
University of Michigan Press 109, 111

MINNESOTA
Allan Lotsberg's NEW Fogey Follies 7
Arts Midwest 106
Brainerd Comunity College 110
Cockpit in Court Summer Theatre 76
Dramata Editions 68
Dudley Riggs Creative Services 76
Geritol Frolics 17
Green Earth Players 77
Minnesota State Arts Board 100
National Movement Theatre Association 85

MISSISSIPPI
Meridian Little Theatre 79
Mississippi Arts Commission 100

MISSOURI
Joplin Little Theatre 78
Lillenas Publishing 113
Mid-America Arts Alliance 106
Missouri Arts Council 100
OASIS Institute, The 70

MONTANA
Business of Writing for the Theatre/Dana Singer 50
Montana Arts Council 101
Montana State University 47, 66

NEBRASKA
Grand Generation Center 50
Nebraska Arts Council 101

NEVADA
Jaspers, Carleen 58
Kenneth Scott Vocal Theatre, Inc. 78
Nevada Arts Council 101
Performing Arts Society of Nevada 79
University of Nevada Las Vegas 47, 66

NEW HAMPSHIRE
New Hampshire State Council on the Arts 101
Pontine Theatre 23

NEW JERSEY
Chatham Community Players 76
Creative Productions, Inc. 76
First Avenue Playhouse-Starburst 77
New Jersey State Council on the Arts 101
Prentice Hall 110

NEW MEXICO
Communi-Culture Performing Arts Association 11
Late Edition, The 22
New Mexico Arts 101
Seniors Reaching Out 24
Torchbearers 32
Vintage Players 32

NEW YORK
Armory Square Playhouse 51
Baywood Publishing 107, 109, 110
Cohen, Harold 54
Columbia University Press 110
Drama Book Specialists 111

Drama Publishers 109
Elders Share the Arts, Inc. (ESTA) 50, 71, 87, 111
Filmakers Library 88
Foundation Center, The 94
Garland Publishing 111
Hauppauge Players, The 20
Haworth Press 110, 111, 112
Hospital Audiences, Inc. 45, 112
New Castle Senior Activity Group 22
New York State Council on the Arts 102
Pearls of Wisdom, The 22
PEN American Center 94
Queens Senior Safety Theatre Troupe 24
Random House 110
Rutledge Press 109
Simon and Schuster 110
Staten Island Shakespearean Theatre Co. 80
TCG Books 112

NORTH CAROLINA
Asheville Community Theatre 75
Autumn Players, The 7
Belfry Players 75
Brevard Little Theatre 75
Drama Dears 11
Lakeland Cultural Arts Center 78
North Carolina Arts Council 102
Theatre in the Park 80

NORTH DAKOTA
Fargo-Morehead Community Theatre 77
Greater Grand Forks Community Theatre 77
North Dakota Council on the Arts 102

NORTH MARIANA ISLANDS
Commonwealth Council for Arts and Culture
  (North Mariana Islands) 102

OHIO
Educational Theatre Association 83
Footsteps of the Elders 15, 50
Grandparents Living Theatre 18
Huntington Playhouse 78
Jameson, James & Bronwyn 58
Ohio Arts Council 102
Ohio State University 49, 66
Players Guild of Canton, The 23, 79
Trumbull New Theatre 80

OKLAHOMA
Gaslight Theatre 77
Oklahoma Arts Council 102

OKLAHOMA (Continued)
Oklahoma Community Theatre Association 79
Southwest Playhouse Fine Arts Center 80

OREGON
ArtAge Publications 22, 45, 64
Arts for Elders 112
C.A.S.T. 75
Encore Theatre 12
Kids on the Block, Inc., The 21
Northwest Senior Theatre 22
Oregon Arts Commission 103
Senior Theatre Connections 50
Senior Ventures 71
Southern Oregon University 71
Vorenberg, Bonnie L. v, 50, 112, 113, 115

PENNSYLVANIA
Better Than Ever Independents, Inc. 7
Community Theatre League 76
Full Circle Theatre 17
International Arts Medicine Association 83
Penn State Goldenaires 23
Penn State University 47
Pennsylvania Council on the Arts 103
Pennsylvania State University Press 110
Touchstone Theatre 32
Venture Publishers 112

PERU
Groupo Ferternidad 40

POLAND
Teatr Osrodek Stacja Szamocin 42

PORTUGAL
Older People's Drama Group 40

PUERTO RICO
Institute of Puerto Rican Culture 103

RHODE ISLAND
!Improvise! Inc. 50
Rhode Island State Council on the Arts 103
SPRI Theatre Company (Senior Players of Rhode Island) 29, 47
Theatre Company of Rhode Island 80

RUSSIA
Okhlopokov Drama Theatre 40

SAMOAN ISLANDS
AS-American Samoa Council on Culture, Arts and
   Humanities 96

SCOTLAND
Elements, The 39

SOUTH CAROLINA
Anderson Senior Follies 8
Epstein, Annette Cantrell 9, 48, 56
Greenwood Community Theatre 77
South Carolina Arts Commission 103

SOUTH DAKOTA
South Dakota Arts Council 103

SWITZERLAND
Tanztheater Dritter Fruhling 42

TAIWAN
Uhan Shii Theatre 42

TENNESSEE
Johnson City Community Theatre 78
Tennessee Arts Commission 104

TEXAS
American Association of Community Theatre 83
Austin Scriptworks 52
Bastrop Opera House 75
Extended Run Players 13
Frisco Community Theatre 77
Harbor Playhouse 78
I.E. Clark Publications 54
Rockwall Community Playhouse 79
San Pedro Playhouse 80
Teatro NACE (Nuevos Actores and Cultura Expresiva 32
Temple Civic Theatre 80
Texas Commission on the Arts 104

UTAH
Encore Performance Publishing 56
Utah Arts Council 104
Vintage Players of Provo Utah 32

VERMONT
Cradle to Grave Arts 11
Vermont Arts Council 104

VIRGIN ISLANDS
Virgin Islands Council on the Arts 104

VIRGINIA
Department of the Army Music & Theatre 76
Little Town Players 78
New Plays-Books 112
Paiste, Terryl 58
Playwrights Anonymous 59
Reston Community Players 79

VIRGINIA *(Continued)*
Sixty Karats 28
Sterling Playmakers 80
Virginia Commission for the Arts 104

WASHINGTON
Adamson, Jo J. 51
Mature Talent Enterprises 67
Port Ludlow Players 24
Raging Grannies of Seattle, The 24
Washington State Arts Commission 104
Wrinkles of Washington 26

WASHINGTON D.C.
American Association of Community Colleges 83
Americans for the Arts 83
Association for Gerontology in Higher Education 83
Coordinator of Office for AccessAbility 50
District of Columbia Commission on the Art 98
Independent Sector 94
Museum One Publications 110
National Assembly of State Art Agencies 111
National Association for Poetry Therapy (APT) 85
National Association for Drama Therapy (NADT) 85
National Coalition of Arts Therapies Association 85
National Council on the Aging 85, 111
National Theatre Community Vaudeville 45
Nomads Theatre Workshop 79
Presidents Committee on the Arts and Humanities, The 111
Very Special Arts 85

WISCONSIN
Bi-Folkal Productions 53, 113
Foxettes RiverCity Theater -
    Silver Foxettes and the Guys 17
Interactive, Intergenerational Storytelling 47
Sage Players 24
Wisconsin Arts Board 105

WEST VIRGINIA
West Virginia Commission on the Arts 105

WYOMING
Cheyenne Little Theatre Players 76
Wyoming Arts Council 105

ZIMBABWE
Chiedza Theater Group 39

Give the Gift of Senior Theatre to Your Loved Ones, Friends, and Colleagues.
E-mail via www.seniortheatre.com
Check your local bookstore or order here.

Yes! Please send me _____ copy(ies) of ***Senior Theatre Connections*** for $24.95 each plus $5.00 shipping and handling. I understand it will take 4 to 6 weeks for delivery.

Name:_____

Address:_____

City:_____ State:_____ Zip:_____

Phone: _____ Email:_____

❑ Visa ❑ M/C Card No._____

Exp. Date: _____ Signature: _____

Checks and money orders payable in U.S. dollars only. International orders add $5.00.
Please mail to: *ArtAge Publications*, P.O. Box 12271, Portland, Oregon 97212-0271
Phone/Fax: (503) 249-1137 (800) 858-4998

Thank you for your order.

Give the Gift of Senior Theatre to Your Loved Ones, Friends, and Colleagues.
E-mail via www.seniortheatre.com
Check your local bookstore or order here.

Yes! Please send me _____ copy(ies) of ***Senior Theatre Connections*** for $24.95 each plus $5.00 shipping and handling. I understand it will take 4 to 6 weeks for delivery.

Name:_____

Address:_____

City:_____ State:_____ Zip:_____

Phone: _____ Email:_____

❑ Visa ❑ M/C Card No._____

Exp. Date: _____ Signature: _____

Checks and money orders payable in U.S. dollars only. International orders add $5.00.
Please mail to: *ArtAge Publications*, P.O. Box 12271, Portland, Oregon 97212-0271
Phone/Fax: (503) 249-1137 (800) 858-4998

Thank you for your order.